The Mother Goose Wars

Geeky and Cheeky
Brooklyn, CT
jessicaamaclean@gmail.com

Dedication

To my husband. For his countless hours of encouragement, cheer-leading, and reading of unedited crap. This book would never have happened without him.

The Mother Goose War

Hansel and Gretel. We all know their names. The story of how the witch trapped them, fattened them up, and tried to eat them. And in the end they saved themselves. Victory and freedom was theirs. All they had to do was kill for it. That was okay since it was just a witch. But what if that is not the whole story?

CHAPTER 1

Once upon a time...

A woodsman and his wife wanted to start their family. They were having problems with this, however, so they turned to the aid of folk medicine. There was a legend that rampion would aid them in their quest. Yes, the very same plant from another famous pregnancy. They went out searching for the rampion and found some growing near their home, or at least they found what they thought was rampion. Neither of them noticed the slightly deeper purple or the deep green leaves. Merrily they picked their plants and went about the task of making a family.

After she gave birth to their first child, a girl they named Gretel, they decided a boy would be a fantastic addition. Again, they went to the same spot and gathered the same plant that had been their miracle the first time. Nine months later, a healthy Hansel made his entrance.

The children grew strong though willful. The woodsman and his wife began to notice things about both of them. They never left each other's side but given how close in age they were, surely that was normal. They also had a way of looking at you: unblinking, cold. And on at least one occasion, their father could have sworn he saw a flash of red in all four eyes when he took away a toy to punish them.

Their mother thought that maybe a pet would help. It would give them something to nurture and love which would encourage those traits to surface. Within a day, the puppy they had been given went missing. The worried couple were too afraid to investigate the reason for its disappearance, though their father could have sworn he had left his axe in the house, not outside.

When Hansel and Gretel were five and six, a tragedy happened in the nearby village. A child had gone missing. They formed a search party and covered the woods and surrounding area. There was no sign of the child. The woodsman and his wife returned to their cottage to find their own children playing with a toy they had never seen before.

"Where did you get that?" asked their mother.

"We took it from Lisle," they responded in unison.

"Why did you take it from her?"

"Because she wouldn't give it to us when we told her to," said Gretel.

"Do you know that she is missing and her parents are very worried?"

"They should stop worrying. It won't do any good. She is never coming home to them again," said Hansel.

And for the second time, the woodsman saw a red glow flicker through the eyes of his children.

Something had to be done. The children had to be stopped. But as much as the parents feared them and knew that they were evil, the unhappy parents could not kill their own children. Instead, they prayed for help.

There was a knock at the door.

An older woman dressed all in blue and carrying a goose under one arm was on the other side. There were no greetings or pleasantries.

"I know your struggle; I have heard your prayer. Lead your children far into the forest tonight. Leave them there. They are in my charge now and will no longer hurt anyone."

Their father led them out into the woods as deep as he could and left them there promising to come back for them after he had chopped down a tree he had seen.

He never returned.

Hansel and Gretel wandered the forest until they saw a piece of candy. Hansel picked it up and stared at it for a moment. And then Gretel saw another in the direction they were headed. Then another. They were greedy children and overconfident since they had never been challenged and began to follow the candy trail.

They arrived at the witch's house about 10 minutes later.

Andrade had been working for Mother Goose for the last 50 years. In her time off, she kept to herself and tended to her gingerbread house. It was the perfect lure to evil. The pure decadence of it could not be resisted by gluttonous children of sin.

She herself had no sweet tooth but still spent her days baking for the greater good.

She loved to read stories of handsome princes and far-off lands and was quite a good gardener. She was also beautiful; long flowing golden hair, tall, and thin. Ethereal would be the best way to describe her.

That morning she had received a visit from Mother Goose.

"I have been watching Hansel and Gretel for quite some time and I am now positive that they are pure evil and cannot be reformed. I'm sorry but I will need you to eliminate them. I know scaring is your preferred method, but it is just not going to work in this case. You will need to take great care, however; they are ruthless and show no signs of remorse. They will do anything they can to get what they want."

It had been a long time since Andrade was called upon for an assassination. Although she knew that it was the only option in some cases, she still felt pangs of regret each time she was called to do this deed. But she was more equipped to handle it than humans were. She could deal with the pain of it and knew why it had to be done. They only saw children; she could see the hatred and evil that would spread into the world.

The myth goes that she ate the children. This was untrue. She had as little appetite for child flesh as she did for sweets. She preferred to use poison for her grim task; far less struggle and it seemed more humane. Fill them up on deadly sweets and send them to bed to drift away peacefully, never knowing what had happened.

There was a knock.

Hansel and Gretel stepped into the doorway of the house after having been greeted by a beautiful woman. She invited them to sit at her table and told them she would bring them some treats because they looked so very hungry.

The two sat patiently waiting for their reward and their moment.

Cakes with bright toppings, puddings with sugared fruit, and shiny colorful candies were all laid out in front of them on pedestal trays and crystal plates. But something seemed off to Gretel. Why was this woman being so helpful to them? She was so kind without knowing who they were. Was it because they were children? Or was there something more sinister involved? You see, one of the drawbacks of being pure evil is not trusting anyone ever . . . it was, in this case, however, a benefit.

As Hansel was about to sink his teeth into a giant sweet, Gretel touched his arm in silent request for him to stop. He put down his treat and stared at his sister.

"Do you live alone here?" Gretel asked the woman.

"Why yes, all of my life. Why don't you eat something and then we can talk about how to get you home?"

She was far too eager to get them to eat. Gretel also noticed that there were two beds here instead of one. Why would a lonely woman have an extra bed in her cottage? And what was behind that door near the oven? Was it a pantry? If it was, why would it have so many locks on it?

"We are not very hungry right now. We ate the candy from the trail. Why was there a trail of candy?" Gretel eyed Andrade suspiciously.

"There must be a hole in my basket, dear. Maybe just a drink to quench your thirst, then?"

"No, we haven't any thirst to quench currently. What is behind the door with the locks?"

"Nothing of importance. Maybe you would like a nap; you look very tired from your ordeal."

Then Gretel formed a plan. She was the brains of the two of them, after all.

"Would you mind teaching me to bake a cake? My mother never did and I would like to learn so that I can feed my brother myself and be useful. After that, I am sure a feast and a rest would be in order."

"Why, of course, my dear. Let me just get the oven good and hot first."

Andrade's oven was great in size. It was the only way for her to bake the repairs that the house occasionally required, as well as the vast quantities of sweets she had to have on hand. You see, she didn't only make poisoned treats for the black souls; she also rewarded good children with candy in their stockings. And there were far more good children than evil.

Andrade bent over to tend the fire in the oven, and when she did, the two children ran up behind her and pushed her in, slamming the door shut and bracing it with a work table. They had never heard such screaming before. Lisle had not even made this much fuss. Hansel found it annoying while Gretel took great joy in the sounds. It gave her a sense of accomplishment and the feeling of a job well done.

Chapter 2

After the screams had subsided, the children decided to explore their new home. First thing first: getting that door open. They searched for a key but could not find one anywhere. Realizing the only place they had not looked was on the woman herself, they opened the oven. Sifting through the charred remains, they found the key.

Hansel grabbed it and excitedly ran to the door. The top lock was too tall for him, so he dragged a chair over and hopped on to reach it. Finally, they would get to see the mystery solved. Then Gretel would let him eat cake.

The door swung open soundlessly and revealed a room of wonder and enchantment. There were hundreds of bottles on shelves that went to the ceiling and a large cauldron in the center of the room with a thick, green substance in it. There were strange items in cabinets. Books abounded. And one book on a pedestal of its own, open in front of the cauldron. Gretel went to it straight away and read the heading at the top of the page: Endless Night Potion. It seemed to be the recipe for a draught that would be flavorless, scentless and would make the person fall into a deep sleep that would kill them in a matter of hours.

"Gretel! What's this?" shouted Hansel.

He was pointing to a crystal ball. When the siblings peered into it, they saw a child playing by a riverside. As they continued to watch, the child ripped the head off a chipmunk and burst into a fit of giggles. Then a voice startled Hansel and Gretel. The child in the ball did not seem to notice anything at all.

"This is Stewart. He is a class four dark one. He is 10 years old and has shown extremely violent tendencies. He is not very smart though. I am assigning you to his case, Andrade. Here are the coordinates." A series of numbers popped into the orb. "After you have finished up with Hansel and Gretel, you will head there with your cottage. Please confirm."

"Please confirm."

"Andrade? Andrade? Are you there?"

There was a long pause.

"Well, clearly Andrade is still busy and this needs to be taken care of immediately before he has time to move on. We have been trying to find him for quite some time. Maleficent, I am going to need you to take care of this now instead."

Then a new voice sounded, this one darker than the other. "Of course Mother Goose. I am on my way now. And I will make the death fit the sin."

The boy stayed by the river and there was silence once again.

"What do you think they are going to do to him?" asked Hansel.

"It doesn't really matter. I want to know why they are doing it. And how many of them there are, and how they knew about us."

"I want to play with a chipmunk too," pouted Hansel.

"I have a feeling we are going to have much more fun toys to play with soon." Gretel's lips curled into a malicious smile. It felt good to smile again.

Gretel saw a light shining from under one of the many books scattered on a table. She moved the book and saw a strange, flat piece of glass. It had numbers on the face of it and a square that said "TRAVEL" in green letters and one that said "CANCEL" in red. She touched one of the numbers and it turned orange. She touched cancel and the number went dark again.

It had been quite some time since they had heard the voice when Hansel called again to his sister.

"Come look!" He was pointing at the crystal ball.

The boy Stewart was still by the river killing small animals as he found them. The most beautiful cat slinked onto his lap and purred. Stewart petted the cat for a moment and then his grasp tightened as he readied himself for murder. Just as he began the twisting motion, the cat began to grow and change. In a matter of seconds, a fully grown panther was sitting on his lap and chest and legs, pretty much his whole body. It snarled and said, "Why do you kill these animals, young one?"

Stewart shuddered and opened his mouth to speak. No one ever heard his last words, as they died on his tongue along with the rest of his being as the panther clawed and tore at him, silencing him forever.

The panther stood, shaping into a woman with black hair as it did so. She glanced at her bloody work and stepped into the river to clean up.

Once again the voice of the woman she had called Mother Goose came into being. With a sigh, she said, "Hopefully the rest of you do not take the same joy in your tasks as Maleficent. There is no need to be cruel or ruthless. It is a grizzly job that needs not be made more gruesome than it is. Till tomorrow, same time as always. And remember, these are not children; they are the embodiment of all that is sick and vile in this world. Be careful, my friends." With that, the crystal ball went dark.

Inspiration hit Gretel. She went back to the glass panel, typed in the numbers of the coordinates from the crystal ball, and hit the "travel" button.

Nothing happened.

Gretel left the room. The house looked the same. No light flashes or rumbling. But when she looked out the window, she saw the river, the same river from the crystal ball and a pile of gore where there once was a boy named Stewart.

"Oh yes, Hansel, we are going to have great fun now."

This was catastrophic. Andrade was missing and so was her house. Daisy, or Mother Goose as she had come to be known, was on the verge of a full-on panic, but that was not an option. She could not fall to pieces or the whole operation would. She had to act.

"What are we going to do, Basil?"

"We are going to do what we always do, Daisy darling. I will watch you have a cup of tea and then spring into action." This would have been a completely normal thing to hear had it not come from a goose that waddled into the room.

"Quite right. I suppose we should get started then."

After tea, Daisy went to her crystal ball and summoned everyone to meet in person at her cottage to discuss the situation and form a search party.

Within the hour, everyone was there. They all had various forms of magical transportation. Some arrived in carriages made of garden vegetables, others on the backs of winged creatures, and a few just walked in. All of the wolves, witches, godmothers, ghosts, trolls, and other supernatural beings showed up on her doorstep.

"Thank you all for coming so quickly. As you know, Andrade and her house are missing. We have no way to track her unless she leaves her house because of the shielding it has, but I suspect we will never see her again. She was sent to deal with two particularly crafty and evil dark ones, Hansel and Gretel. I have sent a complete report on them to each of your books. If they have control of the gingerbread cottage, we have a serious problem. Our crystal balls are our only way of communicating with one another quickly and now they have one. This has never happened before and I am working on a way to block them out. Currently, I have none. They will know where we are going and who we are looking for until we find them and the house. Though this is our first priority, there are still others that need to be dealt with and they will not wait for us to solve this problem. There is evil waiting. Come to me for your assignments before you leave."

"Hansel, stop playing with his remains! We need to get out of here before someone finds him and us. Get back in the house."

"Can we take some of him with us?"

"No."

Once in the house, Gretel set to the task of finding their next location. She found a book on a shelf that was labeled "Active Dark Ones". The book contained information on hundreds of children who were being monitored. Each entry had a picture, coordinates to his home, a personality profile, a list of evil deeds, and a list of redeeming deeds, the vast majority of which were left blank.

A plan was beginning to form in Gretel's mind. She could see it. An army with her at the head. She would not become one of Mother Goose's victims. She would fight back but she would be smart about it. Her brother may have no vision for the future but she did. It would be glorious.

But for the time being, she would have to focus on their immediate situation: getting them to safety, as well as finding a way to keep her brother busy while she studied their new tools and formed a master plan. As clever as Gretel was, her brother was impulsive and difficult to control. He was ruled by his desires and his desires were dark. It had occurred to her on many occasions that her life would be considerably easier if he ceased to be in it, but she reminded herself that he did have his uses.

She had her short term plan. They would go to a forest spot on the outskirts of a small village. No one would be looking for them there, she would have time to study, and Hansel would have other children to . . . play with.

Ina grabbed her pail and headed to the stream to get water for the day. It was sunny and beautiful and she just knew that this was going to be an amazing day for her. It was her birthday. When she left her home, her mother had already been up and busy cooking an amazing breakfast. At the thought of this, Ina's step quickened so that she could return quickly and get her fill of the delicious treats that awaited her.

Something seemed amiss when she arrived back at the cottage. She was not sure what it was, but something was off. It was quiet. Extremely quiet. Maybe they were going to give her a special surprise when she walked in the door. Ina gave a couple of practice expressions of surprise, and when she was satisfied she had just the right one prepared, she opened the door.

The expression of surprise she showed was not the one she had practiced. It was one of horror and confusion. There was blood everywhere. How was it possible there was so much blood and on every surface? Then, everything went black.

Hansel had returned to the gingerbread house and he had brought a cart full of supplies like Gretel had asked him to. There was plenty of food including a fresh, still-warm breakfast. There was one other surprise that she did not expect in the small wagon: an unconscious girl.

"What is this?" Gretel asked her brother.

"I thought I could play with her. You know, poke her with sticks, peel her skin, stuff like that. It will be fun. Kind of like having a friend."

"Or, I could use her to test the spells, potions, and devices in the back room. I am not sure what some of them do and I don't really want to try them out on myself. Will her family miss her?'

"No."

"Is her family alive?"

"It would be pretty impressive if they were," Hansel said with a sly smile.

"Do we have to relocate again already?" Gretel asked with a sigh, already knowing the answer and heading to the witch's private room to find a new location for them.

It was time to start recruiting. First on the list: Nora, AKA Red Riding Hood.

Wolf was on yet another mission for Mother Goose. It seemed he had been busier in the past year than the one before. As soon as one job was done, another one popped up. Was it possible that there was this much evil in the world, or had some mistakes been made in the record keeping somewhere along the way? Daisy wasn't getting younger, after all. Maybe he should bring it up with some of the others, or possibly even Basil. He would know what was going on.

These were the thoughts that were in the mind of the Big Bad Wolf, as he had come to be known, as he made his way through the woods to Grandmother's house. The grandmother in this case was of the dark one known as Red Riding Hood. He had seen her file and the plan was not to kill her, but to scare her. Hopefully, that would put her on the straight and narrow and she would prove to be just a misguided kid instead of an actual dark one. This was Wolf's main gig: scare them to test them out and see if they were truly evil or not. The majority of the time, that worked. It made him proud of his place in this whole business. He saw himself as a safety to make sure no one was accidentally eliminated when they were not actual beings of pure evil.

This time, the plan was to show up at Gran's house, lock her in the closet, dress up in her clothes, and scare the living daylights out of Red, making her think her grandmother was dead. Hopefully, she would realize how precious life was and how much she loved her grandmother, and his work would be done. He would leave and they would find Granny in the closet. Happily ever after and no mess to clean up.

Wolf arrived at the small house and opened the door. He did not like walking in unannounced and uninvited, but it was part of the job. It appeared there was no one home. He went to the bedroom and found the body of an old woman on the bed. She looked like she was sleeping but he could tell there was no breath coming from her. That is when he heard the sound. Someone had entered the house after him. He made ready to run but before he had a chance to flee, an axe landed its blow, then another and another.

The woodsman went outside to where Nora stood. She had dark brown hair, giant, brown doe eyes, and a lanky frame covered by a red cape and hood. She looked both older and younger than her 14 years.

"I'm sorry, child. I was too late. Your grandmother is gone, but so is the wolf that killed her. Shall I take you home to your parents?"

"My grandmother was the only family I had left. What am I to do now? What will become of me?" Nora began to weep softly into her hands.

The woodsman came closer to give her a comforting squeeze. It took him a moment to understand what had happened. He slid to the ground at her feet, still confused to the last breath. She wiped the little blade clean, put it back into its home in her cloak, and looked at the corpse who had tried to save her. Pity. He probably had a family. That wasn't her problem, though.

"Excellent work," said Gretel, as she emerged from the woods behind Nora. "You have certainly proven yourself. I was concerned because your file seemed kind of light."

"I prefer to be creative and stealthy, not showy and gory," said Nora.

"I understand and I think you and I are going to get along perfectly. My brother, however . . . his tastes are a little more theatrical."

"I appreciate your warning and the basket of poison goodies for my grandmother, but why did you help me? And how did you know?"

"I have big plans for a glorious future and I want you to be a part of that. The sister I never had. My right hand."

"Isn't Hansel your right hand?" asked the girl in the red hood.

"Only if I want the land awash with blood, and that is not my style, Red."

"Red? Hmmm, I like that. I think I will keep it. Red. So, where do we start, sis?"

"This is starting to get out of hand. I have lost one witch whom I assume is dead, and I have a dead wolf as well now. I don't know what to do. I have not been able to break through the cloaking of the gingerbread house, and I have not found a way to disconnect the crystal ball. I need a new plan."

"Well, for starters, we cannot continue to let our operatives go out on their own. It's time for the buddy system. Our next course will be to look through The Book of Active Dark Ones and see who might look appealing to Hansel and Gretel. I think it is clear after the Red Riding Hood incident that they are looking for friends. Safety in numbers and all of that. No matter what, it is time to actively do something."

"What would I do without you, Basil?" Daisy said, looking a little calmer while sipping her tea.

"What I want to know is what the others would think if they knew that a goose was really the brains behind the whole operation." Then he emitted an odd sound that was as close as the goose could get to a chuckle.

"Right then, who do we put together? I can't think of anyone that will be excited to know they are paired with Maleficent."

"Rumpelstiltskin might be amusing."

"We are trying to save lives here, not be funny," Daisy said as she rolled her eyes.

"Krampus and Maleficent?"

Daisy spit out her tea. "Are you crazy?! We don't want to let them loose on the countryside together. They will kill everyone!"

"Good point. Let's start a list and call a meeting."

"Woah," said Hansel looking at The Book of Dark Ones. "Look at this! This girl must be really bad. The only entry they have on her is that she is locked in a tower with no door. They have a feeding schedule for her but nothing about what she did. We have to go break this one out."

"Hmm, we will certainly put her on the list, dear brother, but we have someone to pick up before that: a Bo Peep who eviscerated an entire flock of sheep in an afternoon. That is the kind of speed and efficiency we are going to need. I also want to start looking for a large and dependable place to house and train everyone. It is going to have to be huge for what I have planned."

"What do you have planned?" asked Red from the corner.

"An army, sister. Then we will kill them all and there will be nothing to stop us. The world will be our plaything. We will have a family of our own making, a family that truly understands who we are."

"Slow down a little. Let's not get so far ahead of ourselves," cautioned Red.

"That's what I have you for, the little details. I am the big picture kind of gal. Now find me a castle."

Hansel turned quickly, realizing that the chat was over and they were both staring at him.

"Cinderella! Could you come help me? Hansel has eaten a hole in one of the walls again; we need fresh gingerbread and frosting. Really, Hansel, you have absolutely no control at all."

"That's what I have you for," Hansel said, spraying a mouthful of cookie into the room.

"I can't believe this! It is infuriating!" raged Maleficent as she stalked through the woods.

"I'm not thrilled about it either, dearie," lilted The Fairy Godmother as she gracefully swept along. "But I can see why they would pair us together. We are the two strongest in magic and in wills. Who else would be able to stand up to someone as magnificent as Maleficent?"

"Precisely, we should be paired with people who are weaker and need our help, not someone as strong . . . or set in their ways," grumbled Maleficent.

"Listen up, dearie. Mother Goose is sure to have a good reason."

"You mean Basil is sure to have a good reason. How long will it be before the other idiots realize who is actually running things around here?"

"Why do you refuse to just play along? Make someone happy for once."

The pair continued in this way through the woods. They could not have looked more mismatched. One was tall and thin, dressed in severe black clothing, with black hair pulled tightly up under an intimidating set of black horns. The other was short and delicate, in flowing pink that shimmered even in the darkness of the thick, black woods, with soft blonde curls with traces of silver bouncing freely down her back like a delightful waterfall.

What Maleficent hated to admit but knew as well as the next person was that The Fairy Godmother was the most powerful of them all. She also knew exactly why they were put together. It was to keep her reigned in. No one liked the way Maleficent worked, but it didn't change that she got the job done.

"Are we sure that this one is pure evil? A true dark one?" growled Maleficent.

"Yes, this one has been confirmed; however, we don't have to kill him. We are just hoping to get to him before Hansel and Gretel. He may even be useful later as a lure, so let's just detain him instead," The Godmother counseled.

"You know as well as I do that they all must die. Stop being weak and do what needs to be done already."

Just as Maleficent said it, they came to a small clearing with a young boy. He was very small and fair and was cooking something on a spit over a small fire. Maleficent didn't bother with pleasantries or waiting for her partner. She had no concern even for what was on the spit. She turned into a lion and charged in.

"Maleficent! Stop!" shouted The Godmother. Well then, if Maleficent was going to completely disobey and do whatever she wanted anyway, The Godmother was at least going to make it a hard fight for her. She raised her wand and pointed it at the child. She turned him into a lion as well. The two lions circled each other, one black and one gold. Then the black lion changed into a bear. The gold lion changed into a griffin. The griffin struck first, tearing a gash into the lion's hide. Maleficent let out a roar. She was unaccustomed to pain, at least physical pain. These tasks always went very quickly for her.

The griffin took advantage of this moment of weakness and surprise to take flight. Maleficent was quick to recover, however, and transformed into a mighty and terrifying dragon. She took to the air, one great thrust of her wings creating a giant cloud of dust. She wrapped her wicked claws around the leg of the griffin and with one strong tug, flung him back to the ground. Just as she went in for the kill, the griffin turned into a golden dragon.

"Damn it, Godmother! Stop this! One of us could get seriously hurt!" growled the black dragon.

At that moment, the gold dragon sank its teeth into the black dragon's arm and tore at its wing with shining talons. This had gone too far. The godmother shrank the child down into the form of a mouse and ran forward to collect him. Before she had a chance, the dragon Maleficent ate him, then passed out.

When she awoke, Maleficent found she was in human form again, her wounds were healed, and The Godmother was looming over her. She had no idea The Godmother was even capable of an act like looming.

"What did I tell you? We were to take him alive. You are so reckless!" scolded The Godmother.

"What was I doing? What were YOU doing? I could have been killed. How would that help us? I think that out of the two of us, you were the reckless one this time." Then she made an unpleasant and surprisingly comical face. "Yuck! I hate the taste of mouse. As if I wasn't in enough pain already." Maleficent stood slowly and deliberately, testing her limbs to make sure that they were indeed fully healed. "That's it! There is no way this is going to work. We are through. I am never working with you or anyone else ever again!" She turned and stormed off.

"Where do you think you are going?"

"I'm going to go have a word with that duck!"

"Goose."

"Whatever!"

Gretel had been on her way to collect the dark one when The Godmother and Maleficent had arrived. She hid in a tree and watched the whole event. She knew that if they ever had a chance of defeating The Godmother, it was now when she was tired and alone.

She watched as The Godmother pulled a small pumpkin from a hidden pocket in the folds of her gown and laid it on the ground. With a wave of her wand, it grew until it became a carriage, but not just a large pumpkin with a door and wheels. It was grand and gilt, with golden vines wrapped around it in an ornate pattern. There were no horses but Gretel had a feeling that they would not be necessary anyway.

The carriage did not move once The Godmother got in, however. It stayed in its location. Gretel deduced that it must be like the gingerbread house and was probably her main base of operations, which also meant that not only would this be the chance to take out her most powerful adversary, it was also the chance to gain an incredible number of magical items.

Gretel returned to her house and gathered Hansel, Red, and Cinderella.

When they returned, there were now horses hooked up to the carriage for show, Gretel assumed, and it started to head slowly down a road to the east. They got ahead of the carriage and set their plan into motion.

The Godmother was dismayed by the events of the day. She could have found another way to handle all of this if she had just thought it out, instead of reacting rashly. It seemed that Maleficent had finally gotten to her.

The carriage stopped abruptly. She was far too tired to deal with much trouble at this point. She had exerted a lot of magic earlier and just wanted to get back to Mother Goose's house, report in, and rest.

The inside of the pumpkin coach was indeed as Gretel had expected. It was huge, much bigger than one would guess from the outside. It was all decorated in plush fabrics and glittering crystal fixtures.

The Godmother looked out one of her windows to see what the delay was about and saw a girl dressed in rags weeping in the middle of the road. With a sigh, The Godmother stood up and arranged her skirts; she could never resist a sad young maid in trouble.

"What is wrong, my child? Are you injured? Have you been ill-treated? It is your lucky day, dearie. I am The Fairy Godmother." The Godmother knelt down beside the girl in the road, her dress billowing out around her, and put an arm gently around her to cradle her while she cried.

Cinderella looked up at her with giant, tear-filled eyes. "I try so hard to make my stepmother happy. I clean, I mend, I even cook for her. I was so proud of this pie I had made. I thought it was wonderfully delicious but she said it was rancid and that only pigs were fit to eat it. Can it really be that awful? I worked so hard on it." And then she began to cry again.

"There, there. Your stepmother clearly has no idea what good food tastes like. This smells and looks wonderful. Do you mind if I try some?"

"But it might be terrible. I wouldn't want someone as kind as you eating something that tastes bad or may make you sick to your stomach," sniffled Cinderella.

"My dear, I would be honored to try this." The Godmother produced a fork from yet another hidden skirt pocket and tasted the pastry. It was apple and really quite delightful. "How on earth could anyone think this pie is rancid? It's fantastic. Would you like a ride somewhere? It will surely be dark before long and the woods are no place for a girl alone. Come into my coach and think about where you would like to go."

The pair of them climbed into the coach and the godmother immediately settled into an overstuffed chair. "You will have to excuse me, dear. I have had a very long day and it seems to have hit me even harder than I thought it had. I am just going to rest my eyes while you decide where you would like me to take you."

As The Godmother closed her eyes for the very last time, she could have sworn she heard laughter.

"Hansel, stop playing with her body," said an exasperated Gretel as she searched the pumpkin for magical items.

"Why?"

"Because we may have use of it still. They don't know she is dead yet."

"Oh, look at this, Gret," Red said. She was kneeling in front of a chest to one side of the room. This chest contained glass slippers, a gown, and cheese. Very odd indeed.

"That is certainly something we will have to test at some point. I wish these things had instructions or at least a little label saying what they do. We need to figure out that wand." Gretel took the wand and gave it a swish. Nothing happened.

"Hmmm, maybe I need to think of what I want first." She thought for a moment and then swished it again. Red chortled quietly when a pig snout sprang onto Hansel's face.

"I was trying for a whole pig, not just a nose. I guess I need to practice focusing harder." She swished again and the nose was transformed back into a human nose. Hansel was so engrossed in figuring out new, obscene ways to pose The Godmother that he didn't even notice.

"I found you a castle, by the way," Red proudly proclaimed. "It's huge, sits on the edge of a cliff, highly defensible, but there is one small problem. Someone lives there."

"How many someones?" inquired Gretel.

"More than I want to deal with on my own, but not so many that a dragon would have an issue." Red gestured to the wand and then to Hansel.

Maleficent stormed into Daisy's cottage in a whirlwind of outrage and annoyance.

"What do you mean by sending me out with The Godmother!? She almost got me killed!" A sinister dark gray mist with a hint of green swirled around her, illustrating her anger.

Mother Goose casually walked in from the neighboring room. "Please Maleficent, come in, won't you? Have a seat. Would you like some tea? I find that always helps me when I feel upset. As a matter of fact, I will just go get that for you right now and be back in a jiff."

Daisy moved for the door but Maleficent swooped in front of it and barred her way.

"No tea will be necessary, Daisy. Also, I refuse to go along with this ruse any longer of calling you Mother, as if you had any authority here." Maleficent smiled a cruel, sneering smile before saying, "You are not my real mother anyway. She knew how to get things done. Bring Basil out . . . now!"

"Just as I am not your mother, you are not my master," Daisy used her best commanding voice to hide her fear. "I am indeed the one in charge here still, and you will just have to deal with that and me." She had a lot of practice over the years dealing with Maleficent's outbursts but she had never been called out so blatantly before. It rattled her. She wished Basil was with her. "Now sit down, drink some damn tea, and tell me what happened."

"I will not sit, I will not drink your cursed tea, and I most definitely will not calm down. I work on my own from now on. I will still take your little missions, but I will do them how I choose, and with no partner getting me killed along the way. You try to reign me in, but maybe you should direct your attention to others who may botch a job because of a soft spot in her heart for the underdog. Now run along and tattle to Basil." With a swirl of skirts and mist, Maleficent vanished.

Basil waddled from the adjoining room. "I heard, Daisy. No need to repeat any of it. I'm sorry you had to withstand that, dear, but you did well."

"The Godmother should have checked in with us. We need to know what happened."

"We will contact her instead," said Basil as he paced the floor.

"But what if the children hear us? They have a crystal ball too."

"Please stop calling them children, Daisy. Dark ones, monsters, their names . . . just not children. As for contacting her, you are right; using the crystal ball may be dangerous. Let's send someone to check on her instead."

"We could send a couple of the trolls. They were here waiting for new orders anyway."

"Excellent idea. And don't listen to Maleficent. You are wise and an extremely important part of all of this." With that, Basil wandered out, muttering under his breath.

Gretel and her band of misfits arrived at the castle at dusk. It was grand but also old and suffered from neglect. It was probably abandoned until a wandering family or band of gypsies moved in and made themselves at home, just happy to have some form of shelter.

"Do you know how many there are, Red?" Gretel asked as she tapped The Godmother's wand against her hand. She had been practicing and was pretty sure she had the hang of it now.

Red had traveled on ahead of them, using the gingerbread house, which seemed to be much faster than the carriage at getting where it wanted to be. Instead of her usual red ensemble, she was wearing a bright but tattered outfit of a traveling performer. Her hair and skin were also darker somehow.

"They are a band of gypsies. There are roughly 20 of them young, old, and in-between." Red took her shoes off, and as she did, her normal attire and coloring returned. The shoes, which looked extremely worn when on her feet, turned back into the glass slippers they had found in the carriage. "Should be easy enough for our dragon. Have you told him yet?"

"Oh yes, he is really quite excited about it. Good work, Red." Then Gretel turned towards the carriage and shouted, "Hansel, it's play time!"

Hansel bound out of the carriage like an excited puppy. If he had a tail, it would have wagged. Well, he would have one soon enough.

"It's really time? I get to be a dragon and rip people apart and destroy a castle!" Hansel cheered, clapping his hands.

"No brother, not exactly. You don't get to destroy the castle. We need that. That is where we are going to live and train all the other dark ones. We will build our army there and make it our home. We will torture victims and hang their bodies from the walls like pennants. It will be cozy."

"I still get to be a dragon and kill all the people, though. Right?"

"Of course. I would not take that joy from you. I just want you to be happy. Ready?"

He nodded his head, she swished the wand, and a bright red dragon stood where Hansel had been. His tail wagged excitedly and he ran in circles chasing it.

Gretel shook her head with an exasperated sigh. "Hansel, you can play with your tail later; right now, you have gypsies to play with. Come back when you are done and we will move in."

The dragon took to the sky, let out a burst of flame just because he could, then headed to the castle on the cliff.

"So Gretel, are we off to collect more soldiers?"

"Not quite yet, Red. First, we need to send a message to Mother Goose. I need you to tie up The Godmother and prop her in a chair so that she looks alive but beaten."

Daisy and Basil were in the work room pouring over books, trying to figure out who Hansel and Gretel may be recruiting next so they could beat them to it when the crystal ball drew their attention. It was Gretel and from the looks of the furnishings behind her, she was in The Godmother's coach. This was not good.

"Why, hello there, Gretel," said Daisy. "I am Mother Goose. How can I help you?"

"Good evening, Mother, or may I call you Mom? My own abandoned me, you know," Gretel said in a saccharine tone.

"Call me whatever you like, child," Daisy smiled affectionately, a face she had perfected over the years.

"You may have guessed this already, Mom. We have a guest here. The Godmother. She looked so tired and weak after her battle with Maleficent that we took pity on her and decided we would watch over her for a while till she can gather her strength." Gretel stepped to the side to show the godmother bound to the chair with her chin resting on her chest.

"Well, that was very kind of you. When may I retrieve her?"

"You may not have her back until I make sure that all of my future friends are safe. Really, you should be ashamed of yourself, killing poor innocent children. It's just wrong. You were going to kill me, Mom. Well, that is not entirely true, is it? You were going to have that nice lady kill me instead of doing it yourself. Because you know it is wrong! Coward. Just know that The Godmother is in my keeping until I see fit to kill or release her. Stay away from my friends and my soon-to-be-friends, Mom!" With her last word, the ball went dark again.

Daisy turned to Basil and all of the composure she had shown during the chat with Gretel was drained from her as if she had a limited supply and it had just been used up. "Basil! What do we do? She has The Godmother."

"No my dear, she has The Godmother's body. She is already dead and even if she were not, she would be in a moment's time. I'm sorry, Daisy; I know you were close."

"No, this can't be happening; she is too powerful; they could not have taken her down. I refuse to believe it!" Tears sprang to Daisy's eyes and she fell to her knees. "And I let that monster call me Mom. It's disgusting. Godmother can't be dead." She repeated this over and over, rocking back and forth and gasping for air.

"Daisy, I am sorry, but we need to hold our grief at bay until this is over. Right now we need to continue with our plan of reaching all of the dark ones before they do. Even though she is gone, her last mission was a success. The dark one they were after is dead as well. They will never have access to him. Now, get a hold of yourself; there will be time for tears later."

Chapter 3

The dragon had returned to the carriage. Gretel was in an incredibly good mood as she changed him back into Hansel. Things were going swimmingly and she saw no reason that they would stop going her way. It was good to be smarter than everyone else. Now to this castle. No doubt there would be a lot of mess to clean after her brother had his way with its occupants. They sped up to the castle and let themselves in.

Carnage was everywhere but the structure itself was sound. Fortunately, they had a cleaning-obsessed freak to take care of things here. Cinderella took an odd joy in cleaning up the mess of others. She was also strangely creative with body disposal, as well as cooking. Gretel decided in advance that she would not be eating any meat that was prepared by Cinderella for at least a week. She looked at the number of bodies lying around and decided that maybe two weeks would be safer.

Yet again, all of the protectors were gathered outside of Mother Goose's cottage to get updates and discuss what could be done. They had never had to deal with something this insane before and were quickly losing hope.

Rumpelstiltskin was trying desperately to be heard over the crowd, but his diminutive figure posed a problem. He smacked the ogre next to him with his cane to get the creatures' attention, then ordered it to pick him up and raise him above the crowd. It is not often you hear an ogre called a whippersnapper.

Once above the crowd, Rumple made an ear piercing shriek that did indeed get all eyes on him and silence from the crowd.

"I would like to say something. We seem to be focusing on where they are going, instead of what their overall goal is. We don't even know what they want. Are they just killing for killing's sake? Sure, maybe some of them are, but surely not all of them. We don't even know how many of them there are involved yet. There could be five, or there could be 500."

"What do you suggest, Mr. Stiltskin?" queried Mother Goose.

"We need someone on the inside. We need spies."

"Well, that would certainly be ideal, but how on Earth are any of us going to be able to sneak in and get information?"

"We don't. Do you remember a while back I had those Grimm boys show up on my investigation sheet?"

"I do."

"Well, it turned out they were innocent. Just a big mistake. They technically did kill all of those people, but it was not intentional. They thought that the herb they threw in the well would turn it all red, but not cause any harm. It actually did not change the color at all, but everyone in the village died of poison. Now, with the March hare being our bookkeeper, and always a bit behind schedule..."

"Hey!" shouted a small voice from deep in the crowd. People parted to reveal a white rabbit in a vest and top hat. "I have been swamped! Do you think it is easy keeping track of everything the whole lot of you are up to? Well, it isn't. I would like to see you try it, Shorty!"

"There is no need for name calling, March," interrupted Daisy. "We are all very tightly wound right now, and we also know and appreciate the work that you do. Now, Mr. Stiltskin, please go on."

"As I was saying, the boys are probably still registered as possible mass murders. I assume with a tag like that, Gretel will be after them very soon if she hasn't already gotten to them. They are good boys and should be warned ahead of time, even if they don't work for us. The older one is Jacob and the younger is Wilhelm."

"Alright then. Excellent plan, Mr. Stiltskin. Azure?" The blue fairy floated forward. "Normally this is a job I would have assigned to the Godmother. Do you think you can handle it?"

"Of course Daisy. I mean Mother Goose. I'm sorry. I can do it. Really. I promise. I will get them back here."

"No dear, do not bring them here. Warn them of Hansel and Gretel and that they will be a target. Ask them if they would be willing to do some spying for us from within. If they won't, help them find a place to hide long-term, till this is all over with."

"Oh, of course, silly me. I can handle it." She spun around and began to flit away.

"Wouldn't you like to take this with you," Daisy said, holding out a small mirror, "so they can tell us their information?"

"Of course," Azure blushed and retrieved the mirror from Daisy, and again started flying away.

"Azure?"

"What did I forget this time?"

"Do you even know where you are going?"

With a gentle sigh, Azure flew back and took her place in the crowd to wait for her full briefing when the meeting was over.

After the meeting, Daisy and Basil met with Azure in the sitting room of the little cottage. Azure was very excited, as she had never been inside Mother Goose's home. She felt like she was important for once. She only hoped that she wouldn't screw something up.

Daisy handed Azure a cup of tea and sat across from her. "Now Azure, you can turn this task down if you like. We can easily put another person on it."

"No, really. I can do this Mother Goose, just give me the chance. I know I have a bit of a history, but I can do this." The more expressive and emphatic she became, the more tea spilled out of her cup onto the rug and sofa. "Oh my, I am so sorry, Dais . . . I mean Mother Goose!" She grabbed a napkin from the table and began dabbing at all of the spots of tea, and even some dry spots in her exuberance.

"You may call me Daisy. Try to relax a little. Put the napkin down. What use is magic if we can't use it to make life a little easier? Later, I will have those stains out in a jiff. Right now, we have more important things to do, like discussing your mission. This is your first one since The Incident if I am correct."

The Incident Daisy was referring to was Azure's first and only case. Her target was a boy named Jack. It should have been an easy task. She was to trade him some poison greens for his old cow, but she had gotten confused and grabbed the magic beans from the inventory instead. Fortunately, Daisy was on very good terms with the giant that lived at the top of the beanstalk and was able to call in a favor. The Giant finished off Jack and ripped up the beanstalk, but Azure had been put on probation.

"You won't be alone. I will be sending someone with you for protection. Come in, Mr. Stiltskin." Rumple hobbled in from the adjoining room. "Now, since you have worked with the boys before, I would like Azure to be the one to make first contact with them. You will talk to the boys, hopefully convince them to be on our side, and report anything they learn back to us using the magic mirror. Make sure that they know what they will be up against and that they will have to be sly to avoid falling into darkness themselves. If they intentionally kill people, we will have to consider them dark ones as well. They are to find a way out as soon as they feel that they are unsafe or may be exposed. In that situation, they will meet you at a designated location and you will bring them here for protection. If they choose not to take part in the undercover operation, you will help them hide until this is all over or until they grow into adulthood.

"Do you really think it could take that long, Daisy?" Azure questioned with giant, concerned eyes.

"I don't honestly know. But I would rather be prepared for what may come. Try not to be scared. Rumple will help you in any way that he can. He may be a bit gruff but his spirit is true."

Rumple gave a harrumph. "Come along, Azure; we have a journey ahead of us and these two have a lot to figure out."

After the door had closed behind the two of them, Daisy sat down with her own cup of tea and shook her head, staring at the stain on her white sofa. She had no magic herself so she would have to get one of the brownies to take care of it for her.

"Why her?" asked Basil. "You could have picked anyone. Why her?"

"She is innocent and helpless in many ways and they will *want* to help her. Plus, I have faith in her. She can do this; she just needs the chance."

"You are a too much like The Godmother was: always putting your faith in people whether they deserve it or not. I am not saying she doesn't have the best of intentions, but we are dealing with the fate of the whole world here. You sent a crotchety dwarf and a bumbling fairy."

"If you want to lead this thing, Basil, by all means, do it. I do not enjoy this task and would happily hand it over to you."

"You know they would never listen to me."

"Actually, I don't know that. You heard Maleficent. She already assumed you were the one in charge here."

"And she refused to follow orders!" Basil exclaimed.

"She would have refused orders from anyone. You and I both know that. One day, I am going to step aside and you will have no choice but to take the reins."

"Oh really? And then what would you do?"

"Breath, relax, and have a normal life again."

"Those are the boys." Rumple pointed a long crooked finger towards two boys, one standing on the edge of a pond, skipping stones, and the other sitting against a tree, writing. "The younger one is Wilhelm; he is the one throwing rocks. The older is Jacob. They both have sharp minds. I will be here watching and if you need help, just wave me on over."

Azure nodded and glided slowly towards the brothers.

"Jason and Wilmer," she began.

Jacob looked up from his writing and Wilhelm turned to face her. "Are you speaking to us?" asked Jacob.

"Yes I am, Jason and Wilmer Groom. You are brothers with great intellect and pure hearts."

"Ummm, you must be confused, Madam Fairy," responded Wilhelm. "We are the Grimm boys, not Groom. I have never, ever heard of a Groom family here. I'm sorry we can't direct you to them."

Jacob stood up and said, "Did you perhaps mean that you were looking for Jacob and Wilhelm Grimm?"

"Right! Oh my, I can't believe I have already messed this up!" Azure began to pace in small circles while wringing her hands. "Listen, I don't want to scare you boys, but there is something bad going on. There are all these dark ones getting together and I am not entirely sure what it means but Mother Goose, I mean Daisy, says that it's really bad and that a lot of people could die. We need you guys to go under cover because they are going to come to get you since you accidentally poisoned your whole town but they think it was on purpose, and oh yeah, take this mirror to talk to Daisy, I mean Mother Goose . . ." Azure awkwardly thrust the mirror into Jacob's chest.

"Ummm, there is more . . . uh . . . I think I need to sit down for a minute. I am getting light-headed." She plopped gracelessly onto the ground near the tree that Jacob had been sitting under. Jacob and Wilhelm each took a place on the ground on either side of Azure and gently patted her shoulders until she calmed down.

"Now let me see if I have this right," said Jacob calmly. "There are evil forces of some sort, you need our help, and we have to use this mirror?"

"Sort of, oh, I think I need help." She looked in the direction she knew Rumple was waiting and waved her arms frantically in the air.

Rumple was tempted to wait and see what would happen if he stayed where he was, but quickly realized she would just hunt him down. He trudged over to the confused and befuddled group to attempt to clear things up.

"Oh, Mr. Stiltskin! Thank you for coming over. I really need your help explaining this. I seem to have mucked it all up."

With a large sigh, Rumple explained the entire situation to the brothers. "I regret that we do not have more time for you to consider your decision. We just don't know when they will try to contact you. So, which is it? Are you coming with us or going with them?"

The brothers consulted each other behind the tree and returned a few minutes later.

"We will spy for you," said Wilhelm.

"But," Jacob chimed in, "we need something in return."

"How about the knowledge and warm feeling that you did the right thing and helped save the world?" Azure said with wide-eyed innocence.

"How about instead of that, with all of these magical items and spells, you must have a way to keep records or store information as it happens? Maybe a magical book or pen or something?"

"We do have a magical journal," Rumple replied. "You speak and it creates a record of your words. It is, however, not mine to give. It was in The Fairy Godmother's possession when she was taken. If you find it and retrieve it, it is yours."

With a quick look at each other, the brothers answered in unison. "We are your men then."

"Excellent, a little mercenary but still. Now that mirror Azure so awkwardly bestowed upon you is how you will report to Mother Goose. She has the matching one on her person at all times. Just say Mother Goose until she responds and then tell her whatever you need to. We will need to hear from you as often as you can so that we know you are still safe. If you are ever in danger, either contact us through the mirror or go to the crossing two miles east of here and say the words "Golden Straw" and I will be there directly to retrieve you. Do you understand everything?"

"Yes." They said in unison again.

"We are ready and will do what you ask," Jacob said stoically.

"Right then, we will be on our way. Best of luck to ya. Come on, ya daft fairy. Time to tell Mother Goose ya got one right." Rumple padded off towards the direction they had come from.

Azure scurried after him.

"But Rumple, I failed. You had to save the day."

Rumple stopped walking and looked her in the eye. "You are learning. This was all a learning experience. You now know that you need to work on your nerves and confidence. I have had enough wins on my record. We got what we came for. It is a win. You can have this one. Let's be honest: you could use it."

They continued on to the crossroads in thoughtful silence. When they arrived, Rumple pulled out a piece of golden straw. They each held an end of it. Rumpelstiltskin said his name and they vanished with a slight popping sound.

"I have our next target, or should I say targets?" Gretel said while looking at the book in the gingerbread cottage. Even though they had a castle now, Gretel liked to stay in the cottage of cookie. She moved inside the walls of the castle so that she had easy access to everyone and added protection, but she felt that it was fitting for her to stay in her first trophy. Hansel had not felt that way at all and set himself up in the grandest of the rooms inside the castle.

"Targets?" replied Red. She was casually draped over a settee in the corner. Though she herself lived in the castle, most of her time was spent here, listening to Gretel and paying close attention to everything that was going on at all times.

"Yes. Brothers. They seem to have poisoned their entire town. And their last name is fitting. They are called Grimm. They sound perfect. I can't decide who should talk to them though. There seems to be very little about their personalities in their entry. They are mass murders, so maybe they would relate well to Hansel, but they used poison and were very tidy about

it, so you or Cinderella would also be good choices."
Gretel would have chosen herself in the past, but she
did not do that sort of mission anymore. She spent
most of her time in her candy cottage, studying all of
the magic they now had access to. She felt she was
also too important at this point to do the grunt work
of recruiting and training. There were entire days
when the only person she saw was Red. Even her
brother was a stranger to her now, just another soldier
in her growing army. There were 30 altogether at this
point. Some were incredibly dark, whereas others
were just bad. But she needed bodies. She needed to
have the numbers in this. She knew that Mother
Goose had at least 50 magical beings on her side and
suspected there were probably more.

"Why not go yourself? You could use some
time outside. Stretch your legs, get some fresh air."

"I have work to do. I am needed right here
where I am."

"No, what you need to do is make a
connection with your recruits. They will not fight
with or for someone they don't know or have never
even met. There are grumblings going on from some
of the newbies. I listen to them all. They don't know
you or what the goal is. Go recruit these Grimm
brothers and then come back and spend an evening
with everyone. Get to know them. Let them know
what you are working towards. Right now Hansel is
the face of this operation, and he has not made any
effort to correct the notion that he is. Some are scared
and ready to flee because Hansel is . . . well, intense,
shall we say. Others with similar bents are starting to
whisper about Hansel being the one who should be in
charge of this. And then the rest are just confused
about why they are here and what they should be

doing. Honestly, I am a little confused about that myself right now. We started out just trying to protect ourselves but now we are listless. You have also crammed a bunch of murderers and psychopaths in a castle and not let them loose to let off steam. I am surprised that there has not been a riot yet. You are lucky in that but there will be soon."

"Well, that is the most I have ever heard you say in one sitting. Actually, collectively, that is the most I have ever heard you say."

"It's important and needs to be said. I think if I say it, you stand a chance of hearing it, sister."

Though it was hard for Gretel to admit it, Red was right. She had to come out, make friends, and find a way to get them some entertainment that they would appreciate. But first, she would collect the Grimms. It really was a catchy name, she thought to herself. "You make strong points as always, and you are correct that I needed to hear it. You, of all people, must always be honest with me."

"Of course. Shall we go?"

"Let me just finish this chapter on--"

Red grabbed her by the arm, closed the book, and pulled her towards the door.

"Red?"

"Yes, Gretel?"

"We need the coordinates . . . from the book you just closed." After a moment of awkward silence, they both laughed. How long had it been since Gretel had laughed? Too long. It felt good. Maybe she herself needed to let off a little steam, too. She grabbed the book and the tiny pumpkin and headed outside. Before she left, she used The Godmother's wand to cast a magic seal on the gingerbread house.

She trusted no one here. Well, except maybe Red, but even that made her uncomfortable.

Gretel put the pumpkin down on the ground, said an incantation, and it became the coach it had formerly been, but with a few decorating changes since the last owner was in residence. It now served as a mobile command center. Outside it still looked brilliant in gold vines, but inside, all of the pink and plush had been stripped from it. It was still comfortable enough, but far more practical. Where there had been fluff before, there was now solid wood and metal. Shelves that had been full of knick-knacks and figurines were now full of books and tools. The chest that once contained the glass slippers now had food supplies. Gretel had found a great spell that could make a container preserve food so that it never spoiled. It was a small charm compared to what they had done to the castle kitchen for Cinderella. It had a large chest that produced food supplies. She still had to prepare them, but they had a never-ending source of food without having to farm or hunt.

Gretel and Red quickly arrived at their destination. It was not as fast as the gingerbread house was, but it was still a magical form of transportation, and those always moved faster than the mundane equivalents. The targets were by a stream, both leaning against a tree and writing. So they were writers! Good thing that she listened to Red and did not send Hansel.

The boys looked up as the carriage approached with a guarded and cautious surprise. She forgot sometimes how this all seemed when it was new. Houses made of candy, horseless carriages made out of golden pumpkins, magic wands. It was a lot to take in at once. And the new knowledge that the mother of a goose - though she really had no idea if there was any goose at all or if that was just a really odd nickname - was trying to kill them. It was a lot to swallow.

While thinking of all of this, Gretel resolved to find the most charismatic dark one in her collection and train them to be the full time welcoming committee. She certainly did not want Hansel going out to do this anymore. As a matter of fact, she had quite a few positions she was going to create. They need order. Meeting with all of them tonight would help her figure out who would be best for what jobs. She should sit down and make a list right now. She walked to her desk and sat down with pen and paper and began writing.

Red cleared her throat at the door. "Forgetting something?"

She had gotten ahead of herself again. "Let's get this over with."

They walked over to the boys and Gretel began. "This is going to sound very unbelievable, but you are being hunted by a woman who goes by the name of Mother Goose." She continued with the whole speech and ended with inviting them to take up residence at the castle.

"We have in fact already had a visit from two of Mother Goose's henchmen: a clumsy fairy and an angry little dwarf," said Jacob.

"Really?" said Gretel in complete shock. "How is it that you are still alive to tell the tale? Did you kill them?"

"We did not. They wanted us to be spies for them and we agreed," said Jacob.

"For a price!" Wilhelm chimed in.

"It is very daring of you to tell me this. Why would you tell me your plans, and what was your price?"

"Well," Jacob began. "We would rather work for you. Who knows what they will do to us when they are done with us; we are, after all, still murderers. They would never let us live. But if we play along for now, we may be able to get information flowing in the opposite direction and learn about them, or even feed them bad information when needed. As for the price, they promised us something they don't even have to give, but you do. That coach had a journal in it, a magic one that records the words you say instead of having to write it out. That would be of value to us because we are writers."

"You are writers? I thought you were murderers," said Red with a raised brow.

"Everyone needs a hobby," stated Wilhelm.

"So, we give you this book, and you spy for us?" Gretel asked. "What keeps you from spying on us for them?"

"Self-preservation," said Jacob.

"Wise," Red responded with a nod.

"Welcome to our merry band of rebels, Grimms," said Gretel cheerily. "You can also help me by entertaining the troops at the castle. They are getting bored with being cooped up. You shall tell them gory tales tonight at our feast. Also, I very much like your name. Grimm. Is it your original one, or did you make it up like one of your stories?"

"It is ours by birth. And we will be happy to tell a macabre tale or two at the feast this evening," Jacob said with a wink at Red. This confused her. He was roughly her age, 14 or so she guessed, but she had never had anyone notice her, let alone flirt with her. What game was he playing?

They loaded into the carriage and were away in a flash, barreling towards the castle and sharing lively and fun conversation. Gretel could not remember the last time she had this much fun. Maybe the feast tonight would not be so bad.

Chapter 4

Once back in her cottage within the castle grounds, Gretel began making her list of positions that were needed. They would need the recruitment specialist, an inquisitor, a captain who can train them in fighting and whip them into shape, and she, of course, would be the one in charge of research and development, as well as strategy and the whole army.

It was time to go to the party and introduce herself.

She entered the great hall and headed straight to the throne at the back of the room. Hansel had already taken the one on the left and Red was standing to the right of and slightly behind the remaining one. Gretel turned and stood in front of the throne, surveying those gathered there.

"They call us Dark Ones," she said in a large, confident voice that rang through the silence of the room. After a brief pause for effect, she began again. "And perhaps we are. We have certainly all done things that most would consider dark, even horrific. But it is our nature. Our most basic instinct. It is how we were made. Should the hawk be punished for preying on that which is weaker? No. It is in its nature. They, the forces of so-called good, would kill us all. I will not let that happen. I am here to protect you and to teach you to protect yourselves. A lot of you don't know who I am. I am Gretel, this is my castle, and I am the one who can change this world with your help. Things are about to change here. We are going to train, we are going to hunt, and we are going to revel in victories. Many of you know my brother Hansel; he is perhaps the darkest one of all of us. He is my blood and I would do whatever I need to keep both him and I safe. First things first. I am going to be getting to know all of you a little better tonight. Tomorrow, I will be announcing new positions in this army, for we are now an army, and who will be filling them. Then we will begin training. Training for what, you want to know. Of course you do. We are going to eliminate those who have been trying to eliminate us. We will wipe Mother Goose and every last one of her minions off the face of this land. And then we shall make her eat her own goose at the victory celebration while we watch and cheer. Now, let's feast!"

A giant cheer filled the hall with the force of a mighty roar. While the gathering ate, Jacob and Wilhelm went table to table, telling gruesome stories that would make the faint of heart lose their appetite, but this crowd ate it up with a spoon. They were a hit.

After the food had been taken away by a magical wave of Gretel's wand, the party began: music, laughter, underage drinking. Gretel circulated, making the rounds, meeting her fellow dark ones and sizing them up for the future positions. Snow White seemed quite useful but more as a pawn than anything else. She was a little light in the intelligence area. She was beautiful and charming, though. She would be the recruitment specialist.

While Gretel made her rounds, Red stayed in the back of the room, stone cold sober as usual, watching and listening. She saw Jacob take note and head her way. Normally she was uncomfortable at the thought of having to socialize and speak with people for any length of time, but she found herself eagerly awaiting Jacob's presence.

"What are you doing in the corner, Red?" asked Jacob. "Didn't you notice there is a party going on?"

"Oh, I noticed. You may not have noticed, but I notice everything," she smiled coyly.

"I noticed you noticed," winked Jacob.

It went on like this for some time. They laughed and Jacob and Red both thought they felt something growing. Friendship? Maybe. Maybe more.

Bright and early the next morning, Gretel summoned the grumbling, hungover kids to the hall again. The long feasting tables were gone and replaced by rows of pews. Gretel was on the throne with a list in her hand; a very short list, but a list nonetheless.

"I have some announcements. First, that was a fantastic feast, and I am glad that I had a chance to get to know all of you. Second, the officer appointments. The new recruitment officer will be Snow White. The official inquisitor is Rose Red. And lastly, the new Master of Arms, who will be training you in martial combat, is Goldie Locks. She may seem small but she managed to kill three bears while unarmed. When was the last time one of you did that? Snow, Rose, and Goldie meet me in my cottage after breakfast is over. Everyone else, rest up today and gather your strength. We start training tomorrow."

After breakfast, the new commanders, Red, and Gretel all gathered in the gingerbread house for a briefing.

"Snow, you will be in charge of recruiting other dark ones to add to our army. I will give you a list of names each week with all of their personal information and you get them here. You are extremely charming so that should be no problem for you," Gretel began.

"That does seem to play to my strong suits. I am a bit of a people person. Two questions though. Can we call them something other than "Dark Ones"? It just sounds so . . . moody and ominous. Maybe "Chosen Ones" instead?

"No."

"Okay . . . question two. Do we have a name for our army? It would be better if we knew what to call our . . . group . . ."

"We do not. That will also be yours to handle. Make a list of options and bring it to me tomorrow, please. Anything else?"

"That's all." Snow White pulled a little notepad out of her pocket and sat in a chair to begin thinking of names.

"Next we have Rose Red as our inquisitor. You will be taking a different approach from your sister Snow to getting people to do what we want. Feel free to be as creative as you like in this task; just keep it in the dungeon, please. No need to make a mess of the whole place."

"Fantastic!" exclaimed Rose, her eyes alight. "I have a lot of great ideas already. I may need some extra hands, though."

"That is not a problem. You will each be able to recruit your own staff, but keep it reasonable. I still have need of my own resources as well."

Rose turned to Red. "You and I could make an amazing team. Rose & Red. What do you say?"

Before Red could answer, Gretel spoke out. "Not her. She is my right hand and that keeps her incredibly busy. You may want to speak to my brother, though. Last but not least, we have Goldie. Such a cute little thing, but masterful in martial arts. I need you to train everyone. We need to be in fighting shape before the big battle."

"The big battle?" asked Goldie.

"Of course. There is always one massive battle to decide the fate of those in conflict. I see no reason why this should be any different. Now, you all have your tasks. I will want to meet every morning before breakfast to discuss the days' plans and to pass any new information I have on to you. Any other questions?"

"Why should we do all of this for you?" asked Rose.

"For freedom when it is all over. So that you will never be hunted again."

"Fair enough. See you in the morning." All but Red and Gretel left the house.

"Do you think they will follow your orders, Gret? Do you trust them?"

"I have said this before Red; I don't trust anyone here but you and myself. We are all murderers, liars, cheats, and thieves. Do you trust them, Red?"

"Not one of them. That includes you and me." And with that, Red exited, leaving Gretel alone to dwell on what that meant.

Rumple and Azure were off again. Out to find another dark one to eliminate before they had a chance to join forces with Hansel and Gretel. Azure was nervous, very nervous. She had never been sent on a mission that involved killing anyone. She had bumbled every task to this point; how much worse would it be when it was something so serious as taking a life? Fortunately, Rumple would be there as well. He had been surprisingly patient with her on their last mission, and in the days since, he had taken her under his wing and tried to help make her a more successful agent for Mother Goose. Today would be a test run of her new skills. Daisy had decided, with Rumpelstiltskin's input, that Azure should not be allowed on missions that involved a lot of talking to people.

They walked in silence to a small house. There was nothing unusual about it at all. The birds were chirping and the woodland creatures frolicked and went about their business, gathering nuts and chattering away. It was a lovely day. Smoke curled from the chimney of the small home and the smell of chicken stew wafted around them.

"Let me go in first," said the old dwarf to his protégé, "just in case his parents are home."

Azure nodded and took a few steps back.

"I will signal you when it is time to come in. You have the spindle?" asked Rumple. And Azure nodded and held it up to show him she did indeed. "Good."

Rumple approached the hovel and knocked. He waited. No response. He tried again. Still no response. The door was slightly ajar so he gently pushed it open and peered inside. Seeing no obvious danger, he walked in. The house was indeed empty.

The fire was still burning and the kettle was bubbling away, full of the chicken stew they had smelled earlier. Nothing appeared disheveled or out of place. Maybe they had just stepped out for a few minutes to get some water or relieve themselves. At least there was clearly no danger in here. He would go tell Azure to come inside to wait with him.

When Rumple exited the dwelling, he was dismayed to find that the blue fairy was not where he had left her. That daft girl. He had expressly told her to stay there until he gave her the signal. The more he searched, the more concerned he became. There was no way that she would have left on her own. But she was clearly gone. Then he noticed a small note lying on a bush.

"To Whom It May Concern:
We have the blue fairy and we will soon know all of your secrets. Don't bother coming for her. We will send her back to you when we are done.
Hugs and Kisses,
"The Children's Rebellion"

So now they had a name and Azure. He had better get word to Daisy and Basil fast.

"How long do you think she will be asleep?" Hansel asked as he poked at the blue fairy with a pudgy finger.

"Forever, unless I cure it. That spindle is potent," Gretel replied, pulling her nose from one of the many books she had in the study of the gingerbread house. "It looks like a kiss will awaken her, but not just any kiss; it has to be from a prince. Fortunately, we happen to have one of those. Hansel, please go get Prince Charming for me."

Hansel hopped up and waddled out the door.

"Why do we even need to wake her up at all?" Snow asked. She had been the one to catch her while she was on a recruiting mission. "She is no harm to us this way. We could just throw her in the dungeon. No need to even lock the cell."

"Because we want to find out what she knows. She can't answer questions this way, can she? Which reminds me, bring me your sister. This is now her department. Well done catching her, though. Well done indeed."

After Snow had left them alone, Red walked over to Azures' sleeping form and brushed a stray hair from her face. "She is rather pretty, isn't she? You don't often expect the pretty ones to be murders."

"The same could be said about you. Can you believe how dense Snow can be? Just let her sleep? How would that be useful at all? We need to know what she knows."

Hansel barged into the room with an extremely dashing young man. You could practically see a twinkle when he flashed his rakish smile. Sixteen and full of bravado already.

"You needed a handsome prince?" questioned Charming in the most arrogant way possible.

"I don't recall specifying handsome, but prince, yes. I need you to kiss that fairy. She is easy on the eyes so this should be no chore for you," Gretel replied flippantly.

"And what if I choose not to? These lips are not just for anyone. My kisses are special; magical, some have said."

"You are, of course, free to leave at any time. You are not a hostage. As a matter of fact, according to your chart, you don't have that bad a history. The only reason you were allowed entry was because you begged us. You feared for your life that they would come after you. Your only past transgression was forcing yourself on a commoner. That's right, a commoner would not have you willingly. A sleeping girl should be right up your alley. But please, if you think the task is beneath you, do go. You know the way out."

Charming was stunned to silence. She had called him out as being relatively useless, except for this one task. She was right, of course. The fairy girl was very pretty, though. "Fine, I shall do the task. Where may I take her for some privacy?"

"You do not require privacy in this; just kiss her and be on your way. Maybe later when we have finished with her, you can have her back as a personal plaything, but for now . . ." Gretel raised her voice and an eyebrow while nodding towards Azure. The prince leaned over and gave her a brief kiss on the mouth, then left the room as quickly as possible.

Azure's eye slowly fluttered open. "Rumple? What happened?" As her vision cleared, she could see that she was not in the woods, but in Andrade's cottage. For a brief moment, hope washed over her. It left just as quickly when she saw Hansel and Gretel leaning over her. She tried to jump up but she was well bound and could not move.

"Just relax, fairy. You are under our care now. We have some questions for you," said Gretel, in the closest thing she could to a soothing tone. "This can be very easy if you just answer me honestly and without struggle. Can you do that?"

"Are you Gretel? Are you the one that killed my friend Andrade?" There were already tears in Azure's eyes.

"I am and I did. You should know, it was not quick. She screamed so loudly while she burned. I did not know someone could take that long to burn to death, but it was my first time. Now that you know who I am, who are you? What is your name?"

"No, I won't tell you anything," Azure said defiantly. She was mustering all of the courage she had. Daisy would not let her die here. And Rumple knew she was missing. They would come and save her. She just had to be strong until then. This was one time she would not be the weak link.

"Well, that is a shame then. I suppose you will be taking up residence in the dungeon. Meet Rose Red. You will be in her charge from now on. You really should have just answered my questions. I hate making a mess. Good day to you." Gretel returned to the book she had been reading as Azure was carried out of the house and relocated to her new cell in the dungeon.

Daisy's eyes flew to her front door as it burst open. A very animated Rumpelstiltskin rushed through it. "Daisy, where is Basil? We need him now!"

"Calm down, Mr. Stiltskin. Take a nice deep breath and have a seat. I am sure he is around."

"Shut up Daisy and bring Basil here now! There is no time for this charade!"

Basil waddled into the room as quickly as his little goose legs could carry him. "What is going on?"

"They have Azure. It's my fault. I left her alone for two minutes and then she was gone and this note was left behind." He laid the note on the floor where Basil could read it easily.

"Oh dear, dear, dear. This does not sound good at all."

"What is going on?" Daisy queried, exasperated by the lack of respect that Rumple had shown her.

"Be a dear and make some tea, please," commanded Basil.

"No! I am done making tea and busying myself with mundane activities. I will be informed from now on and I will have a say in things!" Daisy stomped her foot. Had the situation been different, it would have been comical.

"Azure is captive. They will surely torture and kill her. There is nothing you can do right now but slow us down. Make the tea. This is not the time to make your great stand," Basil said firmly.

Daisy flopped down onto the settee like a petulant child and refused to move.

"We don't know where they are, so what do we do?" asked Rumple to get back on track.

"We don't know where they are but we do know someone on the inside. We should be getting a message from them any time now. Until then, stay here with us. I would offer you some tea, but . . ." Basil cast a disdainful glare at Daisy.

A mere half hour later, a small mirror sitting on the table began to glow. Daisy picked it up. She had somewhat recovered from her sulk, as proven by the steaming cups of tea on the side table. "Hello, dear. It is good that you contacted us. Are you well?"

"Get to the important things, ya daft woman! Skip the pleasantries!" Rumple shouted from the corner.

"You will have to excuse him, Wilhelm. He is on edge because the dark ones seem to have absconded with Azure. You know her. Blue fairy. You haven't happened to have seen her, have you?"

The little image of Wilhelm Grimm in the mirror replied, "That is why I am contacting you. They definitely have her. She is locked in the dungeon but we can't get to her. Rose Red has become head inquisitor and only those who are on her very small team are allowed anywhere near there. She looked okay when I saw them carrying her in there, though. Also, there are commanders now and they are calling themselves an army. The Children's Rebellion."

"Who are the commanders, Wilhelm?"

"Snow White is the head of recruiting. She is the one who caught Azure. Rose Red, as I already said, is the inquisitor. And Goldie Locks is in charge of training everyone in martial combat. Gretel has made herself a sort of queen, but no one really trusts her because they don't know her. Hansel is the worst person I have ever met. He has no redeeming qualities at all. Oh, and before I forget, Red is the right hand of Gretel. She is quiet and smart. Jacob seems to be getting close to her. This could really help us out. I believe he is with her right now actually. I need to get back before dinner; we have become the official bards and they will notice if either of us are missing for long."

"Before you go, we need a location," Daisy said calmly. Jacob did not know the exact location, but instead proceeded to describe the castle and countryside in as much detail as he could, which was all they needed.

"I know that place," stated Rumple.

"Hurry back so they do not miss you. This has been incredibly useful and helpful information. We will do everything we can to keep Azure safe; meanwhile, you and your brother keep yourselves safe."

The mirror went dark.

"Well, at least we know she is safe," said Daisy, sipping her tea. "A good night's sleep for all of us and then off to rescue her bright and early in the morning."

"What are you talking about? We need to go now."

"Please take a breath, Rumpelstiltskin," Basil said calmly. "There is nothing that we can do tonight. They are unlikely to really do anything to her until tomorrow and to be quite blunt if we went there now, we would lose. We have no plan. I suggest we get in touch with the troll king and have him send a raiding party to the castle. They are far more equipped than we are to handle combat. Daisy, please contact him now and send him on his way. Mr. Stiltskin, please drink this, go to the guest quarters, and sleep. It has been a long day." Basil nudged a potion bottle on the table towards the dwarf.

"Fine! But I won't like it, and if anything happens to that poor little fairy, I am holding you personally responsible."

"I'm done with her." Rose proclaimed to Gretel at the morning meeting in her quarters.

"Already? I assume you mean that fairy, and not some other person you have been torturing," Gretel said with surprise.

"Yes."

"Well, what information did you get from her? Tell me everything," Gretel said, anxiously leaning forward in her seat.

"Nothing. I got nothing at all from her," grimaced Rose.

"Well then, clearly you are not done with her, Rose. I suggest you get back to work."

"You don't understand. I am very good at this. She is not giving me anything at all. All she does now is stare with her remaining eye. I did truly terrible things to her, and I let Hansel do terrible things to her. She is not saying anything. She is also useless as a slave at this point as well. I just need to know if you want her for anything before I dispose of her."

Snow chimed in, "I said in the note that we would give her back when we were done."

"That you did and so we shall. Drop the fairy where we found her originally. Take the carriage; you will get there faster. I will contact them over the crystal ball right now, so you had better leave quickly. Don't want you getting caught dropping off the fairy when they show up. Could get ugly."

Rose ran from the room with the pumpkin in hand.

"You are going to give her enough time to get in and out, right?" questioned Snow.

"If she is quick about it," replied Gretel.

"Why are you being so hard on her? She could get caught. She tried her best," argued Snow.

"Why are you so concerned?"

"She is my sister."

"And Hansel is my brother. What's your point?"

Silence stretched through the room.

"Snow, how is recruiting going? Have you made it through that list yet?"

"No. I stopped after I captured the fairy. I will get on it right away, though."

"See that you do. Goldie, how are my troops doing?"

"Fantastic. I was worried that they would have no discipline, but they are doing really well. It would be great if we had live victims, I mean, targets to practice on."

"You make an excellent point. I will arrange a raiding party of a nearby village, something very small to start out. They need to let off some steam and get out of the castle for a while before they begin to turn on each other for amusement. Bring the Grimms but I don't want them fighting. I want to see how they do as the bards of our group, the record keepers to tell the surrounding towns of the horror they will face if they do not provide us with supplies when we need them, as well as maybe a random person to experiment on now and then. That reminds me. Please bring back a healthy person for me to test more spells on. The last one didn't last very long at all."

"You can count on me," said Goldie, proudly puffing out her chest and preening.

"I know that I can," Gretel glanced at the mantle clock. "That should be enough of a head start for Rose. I am going to contact them. You may all leave now."

All but Red shuffled out of the room.

"Maybe you should give her a few more minutes . . . just in case. No point in losing a soldier just to punish them," Red stated plainly.

"Fine, I will give her five more minutes, more than enough time to dump a body and leave. What shall we do while we wait? Oh, I know. Tell me about Jacob Grimm. You seem to be quite chummy lately." Red could hear a hint of jealousy in Gretel's voice.

"He tells very good stories, but I doubt he has much real life experience with the things that he talks about."

"Just be careful, Red."

After a few moments of awkward silence had passed, Gretel summoned the magic of the crystal ball and waited for a response. Finally, she saw the face of Mother Goose appear inside.

"Gretel," said Daisy. "Good day to you. May I help you with something?"

"Oh, I thought I might help you. One of my friends found something that belongs to you in her travels yesterday. I told her not to break things that don't belong to her . . . but kids, what can you do? Oh, look who I am talking to. You would just say kill them, right? A nice, universal punishment for bad children. Well. I have returned your property to the place it was found initially. I suggest you go pick it up before it begins to smell."

Rumple was out of the door like a shot.

"Wait, Mr. Stiltskin!!" shouted Daisy after him. "Let me find someone to go with you. They could still be there and outnumber you. It could be a trap." But he was already gone. The trolls would be showing up any minute to discuss the raiding party plan, but they moved far too slowly to get to Rumple in time. Where was Basil? He would know who to send. The witch! Andrade had not been the only witch on her team. Luna was still available.

Daisy contacted Luna, told her the situation as quickly as she could, and where she was headed. There, now at least Rumple would have back up.

Basil waddled into the room.

"Where have you been?!?!" shrieked Daisy.

"I was taking a swim around the pond." It was a lie. He had been sleeping. Though he was a magical goose and had an extended lifetime, he was old and he was beginning to notice it more each day. He worried what would happen when he was gone. Who would take charge? What would become of Daisy? Time would tell. "What happened?"

Daisy relayed the information as fast as she could, though the story did meander in places.

"You did well, Daisy. Very well. Now we should brace ourselves for the next part. It is clear that Azure will be dead or nearly dead. We have no idea what information they managed to extract from her. I imagine it will be quite a lot since they did not keep her for very long. You should probably not see her when they return."

"I can handle it, Basil. I am stronger than you think I am," Daisy said, simultaneously defiant and somewhat unsure of herself.

"I am sure that you are, dear."

Rumple saw Azure immediately. She was a small pile of blood and fabric and torn wings in a heap on the ground. He hurried over and cradled her head.

"Rumple?" came her weak, tired voice. "Is that you? Please say it is you."

"Aye, it is me, dearie." He knew that she did not have long.

"I finally got one right. I didn't tell them anything. Not even my name. I finally did well."

"That you did, dearie. Daisy will be very proud of you. I am very proud of you. You should rest now. You have had a hard day. You did so well." He stroked her hair and held her until she stopped breathing. Then he wept.

A few moments later Luna arrived. Unlike Andrade, she looked like you expected an evil hag to look: stooped over with a gnarled cane, tattered black rags draped around her to form a makeshift garment, with gray, greasy hair tangled in knots with twigs and leaves throughout. She walked to Rumple and Azure and stood by them silently until he sniffed, wiped his eyes and stood up.

"They got no information out of her," he said proudly.

"Are you sure about that?" asked the crone.

"Aye. Not one thing."

"Good girl. Let's get her back to clean her and give her the respect she deserves."

When they arrived back at Mother Goose's headquarters, they relayed their information and left Azure's body in the charge of the elves to clean and dress for a final farewell that would happen that afternoon.

"Rumple, I am so sorry," Daisy said and gently placed a hand on his shoulder. He flinched from it and glared at her.

"This was your doing! No, no it wasn't. Ye haven't enough wits about ya for it." He turned and pointed to Basil. "This was your doing! I said I would hold you responsible if anything happened to her. Well, from the looks of it, EVERYTHING happened to her. I will take no part in your war." He turned to march out.

"What about the funeral to honor her? Surely you will stay for that?" pleaded Daisy.

"No, I have made my peace with the girl, said my goodbyes. I am through with the lot of you." The door slammed behind him.

"Well, what was his next mission?" asked Luna. "Looks like you will be needing someone to help pick up the slack around here and since I am in fact already here, you may as well put me to work. I didn't know the girl personally so I don't need to stay for the ceremony."

"Here is the file for the next dark one on his list but I won't have anyone to send with you. It's not safe to go alone." Daisy handed her an envelope.

"Clearly it's not safe to go with friends, either."

"Fine, do as you wish. I cannot stop you. Just be careful."

"You don't get to my age without being careful. It will be good to come out of retirement for a while. Shake some of the dust off. Just a quick stop at home for a little snack and I will be on my way."

"We have plenty of food here. Please help yourself," said Daisy, gesturing towards the kitchen.

"Oh, the snack is not for me, it is for this Peter fellow in the file. He seems to have a fondness for pumpkins, and I happen to know a great recipe for pumpkin pie that I think he will enjoy."

Luna recognized Peter right away from the image of him in the magic book. It really was a remarkable development since her days in the field. Everything seemed so easy and streamlined now. How had they all managed to bungle things up with so many resources at their fingertips? Kids these days.

She had her fresh poison pumpkin pie in her basket ready to go.

"Hello there, child," she said in her kindly, old voice. "I seem to have a problem and was wondering if you could help me with it. I think I may have forgotten an ingredient in this pie that I made, but I can't seem to figure out what it is missing. Would you be a dear and try a little bite and tell me what you think?"

"Why, of course, Madame." She opened her basket and as he reached in to retrieve the pie, she felt something scratch her neck. She quickly put her fingers to the wound and found blood on them when she pulled them back. She turned to see who had attacked her and with what. As she turned, she began to fall. The last thing she saw was a girl in a red cape holding an ornate hair comb in her hand. It may have been her imagination because of the poison coursing through her veins, but she thought that the girl looked regretful. Then everything went black.

When Luna awoke, she found that her head hurt more than it ever had, and the room was spinning slightly. Before she had a chance to adjust to her new surroundings, a young woman's head popped into view, hovering over her.

"Good morning, sleepy," said Rose. "I was beginning to worry you weren't going to wake up before dinner. Now, are you going to be a nice old woman and tell me the things I need to know, or are you going to be like that stupid little blue fairy?"

"Even if I wanted to give you information, young lady, I could not. I have been retired for years and years." Luna could hear that her words came out thick and slow.

Rose sighed. "Well, that is going to be a problem then. I wanted to get this all done before dinner because I was going to make you the guest of honor. Oh well, maybe tomorrow. Let's get started, shall we?"

The next morning at the meeting, Rose was filled with trepidation. She would have to report yet another failed torture. Fortunately, this one was still alive and relatively well, so she could continue today.

"Rose, what have you found out from this witch?" Gretel asked with a raised brow.

"Sadly, nothing yet. I have tried so many different techniques but none of them are yielding any result. She says that she has been retired for a very long time, and as a result, doesn't have any useful information for us. I can keep trying things, but I honestly don't believe that she will be of any use to us," Rose stated nervously.

"Hmmm, that is indeed a pickle. Two captors and no information. I am starting to wonder if I chose the right person for the job."

"This time she won't be useless afterward, at least. I have some dinner entertainment in mind if you would allow it. It could boost morale."

"Fine, do it this evening. I am starting to believe that they have some sort of magic anti-interrogation spell on them all when they are captured at this point, anyway. I should research that on my own. It would be extremely useful. I look forward to whatever show you have planned."

"You won't be disappointed."

"We'll see. Now," Gretel redirected her attention to Rose's sister. "Snow, has Peter settled in? Is he comfortable?"

"He is quite well and extremely grateful to you. I do have one unrelated topic to discuss, though.

It seems a lot our comrades do not appreciate the title of The Children's Rebellion. They do not want to be referred to as children. Most of us are between the ages of 12 and 16. Hardly little kids."

"You are the one who came up with the name Snow. And I like it. Plus, we have already used it; we can't change it now, as it would cause confusion. Explain to them why the name is useful. It both makes people underestimate us as well as sympathize. It makes Mother Goose and her team look like the bad guys. Killing poor little children. We keep the name. Your job is to make them love it or at least accept it. Next, Goldie. What do you have?"

"Still doing extremely well, Gretel. We just need real life tests now."

"Excellent. Tomorrow morning. The town of Hillshire. It should hardly be called a town. But it should be big enough for everyone to work out some energy, as well as practice new skills."

"That's great. I will let them know today and work out some maneuvers we can try. You still want me to bring back one healthy person for you, right?"

"Most definitely," Gretel nodded.

"Will you and Red not be coming with us then?" asked Goldie.

"We will not. We both have things to tend to here," replied Gretel. "You all have your tasks and full days ahead of you. You should get started." Gretel waved them all away. After they had left, Red approached Gretel.

"You should go with them, Gret. Same as the feast. It's good for them to see you. Better now, when it is a small unprepared town than later when there is actual danger involved."

"Why do you always have to make good points? Fine. I'll go. But you will stay here and keep an eye on things."

"Of course."

Mother Goose's yard was once again full of people; well, a combination of people, fairies, witches, trolls, imps, and a number of other magical and non-magical beings.

"Things are looking grim these days. This is possibly the darkest time in our history, and I fear it is going to get even darker before it is done. I have called you all here, not to give you yet another pep talk, but to give you a new piece of equipment, a safety that could change everything for us. Each of you come up and take one of the amulets from the table and put it on. There are some in the form of brooches as well, for those of you who already have magical amulets and do not want a mingling of magic in one location. If you are in dire straits, and all hope is lost, touch the stone in the center and say "Mother Goose". You will be brought right back here to this spot. It has only one charge, but if you use it, you will be here and we can recharge it for you. It will only transport one being, so make sure that you do not lose this or you may be left behind when your comrades escape. We cannot afford to lose any more of our numbers. It used to be that magic gave us the upper hand, but it is clear that they have magic and are also learning and experimenting with their own new, corrupted form. We need all of you to be safe for the battle that is to come. I need you to be safe, my friends. The loss has already been too much."

They all filed through, getting their talismans. Basil could not help but see how incredibly morose they all looked. And why wouldn't they? They had not had any good news or happy events in months. The leaves were beginning to turn now. It would be a hard winter this year when it hit. Basil waddled over to Daisy and looked up at her expectantly. She picked him up with more effort than she once had.

"Daisy," he whispered. "We need to have a party."

"What? In the middle of everything that is going on, you want me to plan a party!"

"Yes. They need something to look forward to, to lift their spirits a little. And let us make it a gift-giving party, like the one we have in the winter."

"But, it is just now autumn! Why would we give gifts in the autumn?"

"To make people happy and give them something else to think about for an evening. Instead of the normal exchange, we will make a game of it. Everyone brings something and then we all take turns picking out a gift and opening it. Then the next person gets to decide if they want the gift that person has or a wrapped one from under the tree. There will also be a feast and dancing."

"And when pray tell, do you expect all of this to happen?"

"Tomorrow," Basil said plainly.

"TOMORROW!" Daisy exclaimed, temporarily drawing the attention of everyone with her outburst. She quickly lowered her tone back to a whisper and continued. "Are you insane? How in the world do you expect me to be able to get all of that together so quickly?"

"Magic. We will invite everyone to show up early and make a day of it. They can all pitch in, work together for something good."

"Fine." Daisy walked back to her usual spot she made speeches and announcements from and cleared her throat. "Does everyone have their amulets? Excellent. I have one other announcement to make and it is good news for a change. We are having a party! Tomorrow, here. Everyone will show up in the morning to help out with the preparations, please. It shall be a joyous day spending time together and making merry."

"What are we celebrating?" shouted a voice from the crowd.

"Each other. We are celebrating each other and our friendship. See you all tomorrow morning, bright and early."

Dinner at the castle was always a lively affair. The hall was teaming with unsupervised youths. But tonight everyone seemed particularly excited. Words had gotten out that there would be special entertainment this evening. They all enjoyed the tales told by Jacob and Wilhelm, but tonight would be something different and no one knew exactly what. Even Gretel had shown up.

Gretel stood up and began to speak. "I do not have a long speech tonight. I just want to say that you have all been working very hard and it has been noticed. As you know, tomorrow morning will be a good test of your new skills and a chance to flex your old ones as well. But tonight, we will eat, drink, and have some entertainment. Rose Red has a little something special planned for all of us. Even I don't know what it is yet, but I am very excited to find out. Let's eat so we can get to the show."

The food disappeared faster than usual that night. The anticipation in the air was thick. Everyone loved a surprise.

After the plates had been cleared, Rose had a space cleared near the fire. She had her assistants bring out an iron cage containing a shriveled old hag. She was bruised and clearly had been tortured, but looked remarkably calm for her current situation. Jacob had a clear view of everything and he knew he would never be able to get through whatever Rose had planned without giving anything away, so he slowly made his way to the back of the crowd where he would only have to deal with the sound and not the sight. Fortunately, Wilhelm had managed to get himself out of dinner that night by claiming he was under the weather - he was actually reporting in to Mother Goose. Jacob moved even further back. He was now in the shadows with his back against the cool stone wall. At least no one would see his reaction there. But he was wrong; Red saw everything.

Rose walked over to the fire and used the tongs to bring out red hot iron shoes that had been resting in the back, unnoticed till now. With the help of her assistant Hansel, they forced the iron shoes onto the old woman's feet so that she would dance for everyone.

The children in the room began to clap out a festive rhythm that mingled with her screams and their own laughter and giggling. Jacob could smell the flesh even from the back of the room and it made him sick. But he refused to leave. At least one person would bear witness to her death who did not take enjoyment out of it. And so he stayed till the very end when the screams finally stopped and she was nothing more than a pile of rags on the floor. That is when he finally noticed Red standing a few feet away looking directly at him.

"Tomorrow, we need to talk. In the morning when the other are gone. Gretel will be with them. Meet me by the pond when they have left." And she was gone in a flash. Within a moment, it seemed she was standing slightly behind and to the right of Gretel. Gretel had not even noticed that she had left.

Gretel began to clap and soon everyone was clapping. "That was brilliant, Rose. Well done, indeed! Maybe we should change your job to head of entertainment." Rose went from glowing to ashen at the last phrase. She knew she needed to get information from the next one or it may be her dancing at the next dinner. "Rest well, everyone. Early day tomorrow." Gretel retired to her cottage and the rest slowly drained from the room, leaving Cinderella to clean away the body. It was a pity she was so old. The older they are, the tougher, literally. Looks like stew would be on the menu. She began to hum a little tune while she loaded the woman onto a cart and wheeled her out of the hall.

Chapter 5

Red watched the little army trundle off to pillage an unsuspecting town of innocent people. After they were gone, she wandered over to the pond, taking in the crisp air of the beautiful fall morning. Jacob was already there. He looked tense. It did not really surprise her. She stood at his side for a moment, waiting for him to realize that he was not alone. When he did, he turned with a start and slight gasp.

"How do you do that?" he asked.

"I think the more important question is why are you here? You tell a good tale, but you are no murderer. You don't revel in it like the others do. And you have not brought any information to Gretel. She may be deep in her studies, but at some point soon, she is going to take notice of that little fact."

"Well, I just haven't been in contact with Mother Goose yet. I have been busy here and distracted by all of the fun things going on and getting to know everyone . . ." He was flustered having been so abruptly and bluntly called out by Red.

"Listen, you seem like a nice guy. You don't belong here. You should leave. Take your brother and leave now before they get back."

"I - I can't do that."

"Yes, you can. They won't even notice that you are gone for a while. They will all be congratulating themselves on their victory. Once they notice, you can be someplace safe. They won't care enough about their evening stories to waste time searching for you."

"Why do you care? And why should I even trust you? This is probably a trap." But he knew in his heart it was not. She wasn't like the rest of them. She had never been cruel. "What happened to you? Why are you here?"

"I'm here because I belong here. I was on Mother Goose's hit list and Gretel saved me. That is all there is to it. I am just like the rest of them."

"No, you aren't. You don't take joy in any of this. I have watched you. I have watched you while you were watching everyone else. You are not the only one around here who sees things. You wanted no part of last night either. And now you are trying to save my brother and I. If I leave, will you come with me?"

"I can't. I have to stay here."

"Then I will stay here, too."

"Listen, Jacob, I like you. I like you a lot. I don't want to watch you be tortured or killed either by us or by them. Hell, they could even try to make me do it and I don't think I could. Then I would be right there next to you on the chopping block."

Jacob held her hands in his. "I have feelings for you too, and I do not want to think of you suffering for me, but I have a job to do. I am trusting you right now. I am trusting you with mine and my brother's life. Mother Goose can help us. She can keep us safe. All three of us. I know her. We have been feeding her information. We have an escape plan ready to go and this seems like the perfect time to use it. I don't know what you did to end up on her list originally, but I am sure we can work something out. Just the fact that you are trying to save my brother and I must help."

Red stared at him. No one had ever cared if she stayed or went, or whether she was safe or not.

"It sounds wonderful but I am on the black list in that book. They sent a wolf after me. Gretel saved me. Now they think I killed my grandmother and a wolf. I didn't technically kill the wolf; the woodsman did. I also didn't kill my gran. I knocked her out, killed a deer, and spread its blood on her body to make the wolf think I killed her. And then there is the poor woodsman. I did kill him. I never should have though. If I had been smarter and thought a little harder, I could have found a way to save him. But I thought that they were the bad ones. The wolf had come to kill me after all. I have never looked myself up in the book to find out what it is they thought I did to warrant being in there in the first place. It must be a mistake of some kind. Maybe . . . maybe I could come with you . . ."

"Let's go now. I will get my brother and we can leave." Jacob started walking back towards the castle and noticed that Red had not moved at all. "Why aren't you walking?"

"Because I can't leave. I can do more good here. Maybe make up for the lives that were lost because of me. I can work from the inside. Gretel trusts me more than anyone. I stop some from getting hurt, at least. Give me your method of communication with Mother Goose. You and your brother leave here now and I will join you when I can. I promise. But until then, I will give Mother Goose the information she needs. I will be able to get more for her than you and Wilhelm ever could. This will also give you time to talk to Mother Goose on my behalf. Make her believe I am worth saving. Please."

Jacob had very conflicting thoughts. He knew it was time for he and Wilhelm to make their way out if they were to stay safe. Last night was almost impossible to bear. He would not be able to keep the facade up much longer. And he did not want his little brother around it either. But Red. What would happen to her? He truly believed that she was a good soul that had just been forced into a bad situation, and as far as her file in the book, he could look into it at Mother Goose's when he got there. It must have been a typo or filing issue, or possibly just a big misunderstanding like it had been for him. He would have to find out how they determined who was a dark one and who was not. That was not something he could do from here. Most of the people he had met since he arrived were pure evil, full of hate and perversion. There had been a few, though, a few like Red, who seemed like they took no joy from the torture and the warping of minds like the others did. Maybe there were a lot of mistakes. Maybe he could solve that mystery after they left here and still be useful. Red had already proven that she could more than handle herself in tough situations. And it was true that Gretel seemed to trust her above all others.

"Fine, Wilhelm and I will leave. This is the mirror I contact Mother Goose through." He handed her a small mirror from his pocket. "Actually, I need that back."

"Changed your mind already?" Red quirked her eyebrow and handed the mirror back to Jacob.

"No, but I need to use it before I hand it over to you. Get ready to meet the person you have been dreading."

When Jacob said Mother Goose's name into the mirror, it began to glow and then before even a few seconds, the face of a kindly older woman popped into view.

"Jacob," it said. "I am so glad to hear from you. You look well. I trust your brother is too."

"Yes, for the moment. We need to leave. Would you please let Rumpelstiltskin know that we are headed to the meeting place?"

"Oh dearie, I would love to but he is indisposed at the moment. But fear not. I will have one of our other agents there to meet you instead. And is that Nora behind you?"

"Who?" asked Jacob. "Oh, you mean Red?"

"Red, how . . . expected."

"That is the other part of what I need to talk to you about. She is your contact here now. She can be trusted completely. She is currently the right hand of Gretel and has access to far more information than my brother and I ever would have. I can explain it all to you in more detail when I get to your house. I think I may have other ways of helping you too that I can also explain later. Right now, I need to find my brother and get out of here before they all come back. I am giving the mirror to Red so that she can contact you when she has information. I have to go. Do you know where Mr. Stiltskin wanted to meet us?"

"Of course. Dear Mr. Stiltskin, much like your friend Red there, is very predictable. I will have someone there waiting for you. Now get your brother and go. We can speak later."

The mirror went dark and he handed it back to Red.

"Just say her name and wait for her to show up. It is normally within a few seconds. I think she must keep it on her person at all times. I need you to promise me that you will come as soon as you can." Red promised and Jacob told her the meeting location for her own escape. Then he pulled her close and kissed her. It was a first for them both. Without another word, he turned and ran towards the castle to find his brother.

Gretel was extremely frustrated that she let Red talk her into accompanying the troupe on their expedition to the neighboring town for supplies and mayhem. There were a number of more useful things she could be doing with her time. Still, it did feel good to be out in the fresh air and sunshine for a little while. It was good to stretch. It had also been a long time since she had a chance to be alone with her brother. She went to find him in the group with the goal of some quality family bonding. She found him in a cluster of people all speaking excitedly in hushed tones. She slowed down and tried to be inconspicuous so that she could hear a little of what was being said before getting Hansel's attention. They all seemed to be stroking his ego and pumping him up, occasionally sliding in a thinly veiled suggestion that he should really be the one in charge. Actually, most of those statements were coming from one person and the others just parroted them. That one person was none other than Prince Charming himself. Clearly, he had not let go of their earlier interactions and was still bitter about her comments about his lack of abilities in the feminine department. It figured that the spoiled brat would hold a grudge. She would most certainly have to deal with this as soon as they returned. She did not need a little upstart like him ruining her plans. And she certainly didn't want to let it get to the point that she would have to dispose of her own brother. She still had a soft spot in her heart for him, but she would not hesitate to remove him if the situation called for it.

"Hansel," Gretel said as she approached. It gave Charming a start and he was clearly rattled and concerned with what she may have heard. He smartly took that moment to suddenly develop an interest in a conversation Goldie was having with some other recruits.

"Gretel. It seems like it has been a long time since we talked. I was surprised you came, actually," said Hansel.

"I was surprised myself. Red talked me into it and I am rather glad that she did."

"Yeah, Red," Hansel grunted indignantly. "Seems like she is the only person who is worthy of your time these days."

She had hurt his feelings; he was jealous of her friend. And she could see why. There was, in all honesty every reason for him to be jealous. She had found a new sibling who was superior to him in every way. But he didn't have to know that. It would be much better for her if he didn't think that way. She did not want to have to deal with a possible feud between the two of them.

"I was just thinking about that myself. I miss you, brother, and I think we need to have some alone time. Just you and I. Maybe we could have a picnic by the pond after this is done. I am sure we will be hungry and could use a nice relaxing afternoon catching up. Doesn't that sound nice?"

"Actually it really does. A morning of pillaging followed by a lazy afternoon of food and family. I like it." And Hansel genuinely was looking forward to spending time with his sister. He felt a little empty lately and maybe that was part of it. Maybe it was that he missed her. It had just been the two of them on their own against their parents their whole lives. And then them against Mother Goose, keeping each other safe.

Gretel felt much better about the Charming situation. She now knew that she was catching it early and her brother still put her above all others. Today would solidify that. She would have to remember to give Red a heads-up so that she did not worry about anything suspicious going on. And maybe a quiet afternoon just being a kid and sister away from her books would be fun.

The town was already busy with their daily chores when the band of blood-thirsty children arrived. It was a small village and some kids would probably have to share their victims, but it was a start. Goldie had not worked on a maneuver for this particular event. They were a small community with no fighters of any kind. The plan was walk into town, kill everyone, and take their belongings.

They walked directly into town. No one stopped them, though many stared as they walked through. They did not get many travelers through here, and certainly had never had 30-40 children of various ages with no adults among the lot show up. Gretel found her way to the center of the small village where they held their market. It was closed now, but the villagers had stopped their work and followed the army to the market square to find out what was going on. Gretel climbed on top of a small platform that they used for announcements and punishments and spoke in a strong and loud voice.

"Hello, good people. It is a pleasure to visit your small but lovely town. Rose, that one." When she was sure she had Rose's attention, she pointed to a hearty looking girl about her own age in the crowd. Rose nodded an acknowledgment and made her way through the crowd to the girl. Once she was sure that Rose had indeed seen the correct girl, Gretel continued. "My children, do as you will."

The chaos that ensued was horrific. A short time later, Gretel walked among the dead and observed the activities of her brethren. Many of them were covered in blood and gore. All of them were picking over the bodies. Most looking for treasures or trophies, and some were just playing with or admiring their work. A few townspeople were still alive, but barely. Their tormentors chose to take their time and really enjoy the moment. After all, they had no idea how long it would be before they were allowed out again. Gretel did notice one person who seemed completely happy to be left out of the fight, and in fact, the prince had stayed on the outskirts of the action. He was also still immaculately clean and tiptoeing around messes whether they be blood or mud. She would have to make a mental note of this for his future punishment.

They liberated the town of wagons full of supplies, as well as knickknacks and keepsakes from their adventure. The trip back to the castle was longer than the one to the village, but they were weighed down by loot and the fatigue of an energetic morning. Hansel caught up to her excitedly with something behind his back. She secretly dreaded what had decided was a great surprise for his sister. They had very different tastes.

"Gretel. I found something that I think you are really going to like," he said, with a giant, goofy grin spreading across his face.

"Oh really! What is it?" She hoped that she sounded excited and happy. Hansel pulled a basket from behind his back. He pulled the fabric from the top to reveal a beautiful lunch. Fresh bread, good hard cheeses, fruit. It looked lovely.

"We can go straight off to our picnic as soon as we get back."

"That's wonderful. This looks delicious. How lucky for us that someone else was planning a picnic today as well."

"No, I found all of these things and put it together myself."

"You did extremely well. I am very impressed and can't wait till we get back. Thank you, Hansel. You are a good brother." She squeezed his arm and they continued on their journey home.

Wilhelm and Jacob walked side by side at a brisk pace. They very much wanted to be safely in the care of whoever Mother Goose was sending to meet them before the others even returned to the castle. Hopefully, they would not notice they were missing until dinner when they were not there to tell their stories. That would also be safer for Red. She could say that they had been there all morning and would not be at fault for them slipping out on her watch. Jacob hoped that he had done the right thing by leaving her there. He had doubts, but at least he had a plan to help her start her life again after this was all over. And in the meantime, he was also keeping his little brother safe.

"Jacob?" Wilhelm began, "why did you want us to leave so suddenly and now? Did something happen? Did Gretel find out about us?"

"She has not found out about us yet, but if we had waited until she did, we would not be able to escape at all. We have done our part for this cause. Are you unhappy about our leaving, Wil?"

"Not at all. I had hoped we would be gone before now. I was nervous all the time, afraid we would be found out. I got the feeling that you might not leave without Red, though. I was worried that you had fallen for her. She is a dark one."

"No, she isn't. It was a mistake, just like ours was. I did not want to leave her there, but she feels she can do more good from inside and she is probably right."

"So she is not a dark one, and you left her there anyway? We should have forced her to come with us."

"That is not our choice to make Wil. Besides, I have work I have to do from this side of things to make it safe for her. Mother Goose and the others don't know the whole story yet. And I think there are some others that need our help as well. Others who were wrongly accused. I have a plan though. But first, we have to get to safety."

"Well, let's walk faster. I want as much distance between us and them as we can get. I wonder if Rumple will be happy to see us safe."

"He won't be meeting us. I don't know why."

"Then who is meeting us? How will we know we have the right person if we don't know who we are looking for?"

"I think it will be very obvious," Jacob said as they arrived at their destination.

"How do you know that?" Wilhelm asked. Jacob simply pointed in the direction that he was staring. There was a glowing white unicorn waiting in the crossroads.

They approached it slowly, having no prior experience with unicorns. They did not even know if they could understand language, but there was one way to find out.

"Hello," Jacob said tentatively. "I am Jacob and this is my brother Wilhelm. We are the Grimm brothers. Are you our escort to Mother Goose?"

The unicorn nodded, then lowered the front half of his body. It almost looked like he was bowing. They stood silently, not knowing what to do next. The unicorn looked up at them and shook his head as if motioning for them to climb on his back. The boys climbed on one at a time and the unicorn was off instantly.

The world passed them in a blur, Wilhelm holding tightly to the unicorn's mane, and Jacob holding tightly to Wilhelm. The journey that should have taken hours was over in the span of minutes. The unicorn slowed to a stop in front of a quaint cottage with a lovely lush garden and a small duck pond. Surely this could not be the home of the amazing Mother Goose, the Headquarters of Good.

The brothers dismounted and stood in awkward silence, wondering where the unicorn had taken them.

"Are you sure this is the right place?" Wilhelm asked the unicorn. It nodded and then walked off into the woods. "Well, I guess we should go knock on the door then. You first."

Jacob knocked three times and then took a large step back and waited with his brother. It was only a moment before the door swung wide and they were greeted by Mother Goose herself.

"There you are, my boys. It is good to see you. I trust your journey went smoothly and that you made it to me unharmed." She waved them into the house and they went obediently.

"Now you must be famished. Escapes always work up an appetite, as does being a spy for months on end, I imagine. I can't wait to hear all about your adventures, but first, a bit of lunch and tea. You may head to the guest quarters at the top of the stairs on the right and freshen up while I get our food ready. That is where you will be staying until we figure out what to do with you two. Can't have you orphaned and alone to fend for yourselves after the service you have done us. There are some clean clothes that should fit you and a pitcher of water. When you are finished, the dining room is right through that door," she said, pointing down the hallway.

After the boys had cleaned themselves and changed, they headed to the dining room. They could not imagine how this house had so many rooms. From the outside, it had looked as if it could hold three rooms maybe, but no more than that. The dining room was large. It had a table that could easily seat a dozen people comfortably.

"Make yourselves at home, boys. No need for ceremony today. Normally, Basil and I don't even eat in here. We take our meals in the parlor most days," said Daisy.

"If you don't mind my asking, Mother Goose, who is Basil?" ventured Jacob.

"Oh please, just call me Daisy. I have a feeling we are all going to be great friends. And Basil will be along any moment; then I can introduce you properly. Please sit and be comfortable. Ah, there he is now. Basil, you must meet the Grimm boys."

Both boys turned to see who had entered the room. The new person in attendance was not a person at all, but a goose. At first, the boys thought that the old woman must have lost her marbles, but then the goose spoke.

"Hello, boys. It is a pleasure to finally meet you. I have heard much of your adventures and look forward to hearing more. I trust you will be staying with us for quite some time. But we can get to that later. I am famished and you must be as well."

Basil waddled over to the table and waited patiently as Daisy lifted him onto a special seat that was built to make it easier for him to dine with the others.

The boys took seats to the side of Daisy and tried not to stare at the talking goose. Against all odds, this day managed to continue to grow stranger as it went on. Unicorns, talking geese, cottages that were bigger once you were inside of them, and possibly the most important part of all of it, Jacob's first kiss.

"I would like to talk to you about Red, please," said Jacob boldly. "Uh, Nora, I think you called her."

"Of course, dear. Quite the character, your little girlfriend."

"I don't believe that she is actually a dark one. She told me about what happened to the wolf and took full responsibility for her part in it. That is why she stayed behind now: to redeem herself."

"Well, that is very noble, indeed, if it is the truth. The problem is that we don't have a solid way of knowing if she is or not. Dark ones can be extremely beguiling and convincing. They can make you believe anything they want you to. It does not hurt me in this case to at least hear her reports and measure them with a grain of salt. Then when all is said and done, we can reopen her case."

"Might I ask, how do you end up knowing who is and isn't a dark one? There has to be some definitive test if you are putting someone to death."

This time, Basil was the one to speak up. "Unfortunately, there is no such test. In the end, it is mostly guess work, as horrible as that sounds. I am sure that many who could have been saved were lumped into the dark one list, but the truth of the matter is, the consequences that we are dealing with are much bigger than one or two people."

"You mean one or two children, like my brother and I."

"Yes, my boy." said the goose in a sorrowful tone. "We all pray for a better way, but there seems to be none."

"I am really smart, and my brother is amazing at gathering information. We make an incredible team and can sleuth out most anything. Could we go through the files of past dark ones and those who have been redeemed as well and see what we can find? Any common thread at all?" pleaded Jacob. "If anyone can do it, we can."

"I think that is a splendid idea, Jacob," said Basil, suddenly looking cheerier.

"Do you really think that is such a good idea, Basil?" asked Daisy. "We had talked about keeping them on, but I had assumed you meant as grounds keepers or kitchen boys. Should we really give them access to all of that information? No offense, boys."

"As a matter of fact, Daisy, I think they are exactly who we need. I also have another job for you two if you are willing to help us out a little."

"Of course!" Jacob agreed eagerly, already so happy with the good fortune of the trust of Basil.

"Our bookkeeper is far behind on entering information into our files. That is one of the reasons we were able to use you two. You had already passed investigation, but no one had entered it into your permanent record yet. If you would spend part of your days doing that administrative task and the other part investigating your theories, I would be most grateful to you. You will, of course, have room and board, as well as schooling on both practical education and magical from me. Are you both up for that?"

The brothers looked at each other, then back at Daisy, and said in unison, "Yes!"

Wilhelm asked, "How long will we be allowed to stay?"

"Well," ventured Basil, "I was hoping forever."

This was the best news the boys had ever heard. They would spend their lives learning and writing and solving riddles and studying magic with magical beings that would one day be like family to them. They all spent the rest of the afternoon enjoying their food and company, getting to know their new companions.

Gretel and the others returned to the castle, flush with victorious pride and exuberance. Red was waiting at the gate to greet Gretel. She took a deep breath. Hansel was with her. It was always a chore to talk to him. He was incredibly dense.

"Hansel, I will meet you at the pond in a few minutes. I want to go change my clothes to something a little . . ." she looked down at her dirt and blood caked skirts and shoes, "cleaner."

Hansel looked at Red, then back at Gretel, gave a curt nod and grunt, and wandered off towards the pond. He preferred to wear the markings of his work that day with pride. It reminded him of how productive his morning had been.

Red and Gretel walked together back to the cottage so Gretel could change.

"Red, I have to spend the rest of the day with my brother . . . alone. I am not happy about it, but I caught Charming trying to sway him into a mutiny. I just don't have time for that now, so I am going to use some family bonding to set things straight; win him fully to my side again."

Red held the door to the cottage open for Gretel. "I think that is a very smart idea, Gret. In fact, you may want to make it a regular thing so that you can keep him on your side. Maybe not an entire day every time, but at least an hour or two."

"You're right. You always are." Gretel removed her mud and gore-encased shoes and took a few long slow breaths to prepare for her afternoon with her brother.

"What are you going to do about Charming?"

"I am not sure yet. He doesn't even belong here in the first place. Do you have any ideas?"

"Not at the moment."

"For now, keeping him locked up in the dungeon without access to a mirror or female companion will probably suffice as torture until we can come up with something better."

"I'll go talk to Rose about it this afternoon while you have family time if you like."

"That sounds great. Then tonight after dinner, we will have him taken away in front of everyone. No explanation though. I don't want anyone thinking there was ever a weakness in my control of this whole thing. I think having him removed at dinner without a reason will still send a strong message to the rest of them of who is in charge and that disloyalty will not be tolerated."

Gretel was dressed and clean and ready to head out. "I suppose it is time for me to go have . . . fun." She said the last word with disgust.

"Maybe you will have fun, Gret. Just relax and enjoy the day. I have everything under control here."

Gretel smiled at her friend with full confidence that the things she had asked Red to handle would be done and done efficiently. She was so lucky that there was at least one other smart person for her to confide in and share her burden.

After Gretel had left, Red headed out herself to find Rose. She had at least managed a stay of execution for Charming, whether he deserved it or not. That had to look good for her later with Mother Goose when she would be judged again. Hopefully, Jacob would be able to figure something out by then. She thought of the kiss. It had been her first and so sudden and unexpected that she did not get to fully enjoy it. Or say goodbye to Jacob as he fled. At least he was safe now. She fingered the designs on the small mirror in her pocket. It would be so easy for her to leave. All she had to do was ask to be rescued. Gretel would be away all afternoon. She could slip out and see him again and they would both be safe.

But she had not yet proven herself to be worthy of being safe and happy, not only to Mother Goose, but to herself as well, and of course for Jacob. She let the mirror fall fully back to the bottom of her pocket and walked on to the dungeon. Though they had just returned from their quest and were hungry and tired, she knew that Rose would be there, probably seeing to the accommodations of Gretel's newest experiment. Rose was not in great standing right now and spent most of her free time trying to find ways to claw herself back up the ranks again.

When Red arrived at the dungeon, she found that she had been correct about everything. Rose was closing a cell door on a chubby girl who was clearly terrified. Red wished she could say something comforting to her or give her a visual cue of hope like a small smile or wink, but she couldn't. Not only because she didn't want to risk being spotted doing it, but because there was no hope for this poor girl. It seemed almost cruel to betray her by giving her any false hope. She would die here and probably in a horrible fashion. If she was lucky, it would be from the very first magic item or spell that Gretel used on her. But that was unlikely.

"Rose, Gretel has a job for you. This is just between the two of us and one other of your assistants to aid you when the task is to be done."

"Of course, what is it?" Rose asked eagerly. She leaned in expectantly, waiting for the orders that would win her favor.

"Prince Charming has become an issue."

"I knew he would be a problem eventually. I am surprised that it took this long to catch up to him. What did he do this time?"

"That isn't important for either of us to know. What is important right now is that you take care of him. At dinner tonight when Gretel signals to you, you and your assistant - preferably not Hansel - will take Charming and lock him up down here. Make a big show of it, if you can. He is to be kept safe but confined for now until Gretel figures out what to do with him. If you have any creative and appropriate punishments for him, please let me know. We can decide whether it will be a good one to bounce off Gretel or not. I know you could use the points right now. This should be pretty easy and buy you some time to find ways to make her like you again."

"Red, you have to know that there was nothing I could have done to make either of those two talk. I think they have a magic spell or talisman that keeps them from being able to talk no matter how much torture they receive. You would not believe the things I did to them. I made myself sick a few times."

"I know, Rose. But that is in the past and is neither here nor there. We have to deal with what is in front of us now. I like you and I would like you to be here. I want to help you and I will. Now I have some things to tend to and you have to figure out the most obnoxious way to bring Charming down. Have fun planning."

"Thank you, Red. It's good to know I have at least one friend other than my sister here. Hansel likes me too but he would sell me out in a heartbeat. Actually, he would sell anyone out, even his own sister. But you didn't hear that from me. OK, Red?"

Red nodded, smiled what she hoped was a comforting smile, turned, and left.

Later that evening at dinner, Gretel stood and drew everyone's attention for yet another one of her speeches.

"You all performed wonderfully today. I hope you enjoyed yourself and were able to let off some steam, as well as try out some of the new skills you have been developing. Some interesting things came to light for me today during our outing. There are some who do not belong here, who are here for the wrong reasons. This will not be tolerated. I suggest if any of you are here for the wrong reasons, you leave in the night tonight when no one is looking. You will be found out; make no mistake. As a matter of fact, we already know who some of you are. Rose, please relocate our resident Prince to his new lodgings. Make sure he is incredibly uncomfortable."

Charming's head jerked up and his eyes flew away from the cleavage he had been intensely interested in moments before. "What!?!? What's going on?" He was already on his feet and being dragged to the end of the hall where a cage was sitting. Where had that cage come from? Had it always been there? What had he done? Where were they taking him? Were they going to kill him, or worse, scar him horribly? He desperately wanted to be back home in his kingdom. He would be shamed, loathed even, for his past indiscretions; but he would be safe, at least.

They threw him in the cage which was on a dolly and wheeled him from the room. There was stunned silence.

"Well, now that the nasty business is taken care of, let's eat and then have some entertainment. Stories from our brothers, I should think." But when Gretel scanned the room to find them, they were missing. Curious. This was something that she would have to have Red look into. She motioned for Red to lean closer.

"Where are the Grimms?" she asked.

Red made a show of looking around the room to see if she could spot them, even though she knew they were safely in the home of Mother Goose. "I don't know. I will see if I can find out. Maybe they are taken ill, but they both looked healthy enough when I saw them earlier today. I was actually fairly surprised that they didn't go with you guys, if not to participate, at least to document the experience. It seems like a great adventure for a bard or two to have witnessed."

"Hmmm, that is curious indeed. Something worth investigating."

"I will get on it right now." Red left the table and headed into the darkened hallway and towards the room the brothers had shared.

It was a quiet journey through the empty castle. With everyone in the main hall except for her and Charming and his escort to the dungeons, it gave her time to reflect on the day and on Jacob. When she arrived at their room, she hesitated. What would she find when she entered? Would it stir emotions that she was trying to suppress, at least for the time being?

She pushed the door open and entered. She found it much the way it had been when they resided there. It was as messy as a boy's room usually is. The journal was gone. It would have been foolish to think that they may have left it behind, but part of her had hoped that he had left it so that she could read his writing and pretend he was there talking to her, telling her stories. Perhaps she could even see if he had written about her. She searched the room, trying to pretend that it was just to make sure they did not leave anything incriminating behind, but she was really hoping to find something for her, anything he may have left. And then she found a small scrap of red paper tucked away in a shirt pocket. She unfolded it and it simply said, Nora. It was enough. It was a sign that he had thought of her and had taken the time to leave her something to cling to. She folded it quickly and put it with the mirror in her pocket. That was it. She made sure that the hall was clear and no one was coming and pulled out the mirror. Taking a deep breath, she spoke Mother Goose's name and waited.

"Hello, Nora. How can I be of service?"

"Hello. I just wanted to make sure that Jacob and Wilhelm got there safely."

"Yes, they did. In fact, we are just preparing for a gathering, dear. A little celebration and I do have to be on my way now."

"Of course, but before you go, Gretel found Prince Charming trying to get Hansel to mutiny. She had him thrown in the dungeon to await punishment. I don't know when or what it will be, but I will keep you up-to-date."

"Such a horrid boy, but not a dark one. Thank you and please keep me informed. I really must go now."

And the mirror went back to being a mirror. Mother Goose had looked extremely festive. She probably should have warned her about the gift that Gretel had sent along for their little celebration. It was one of the last pieces of information that the Grimms had passed along to Gretel to keep up appearances before leaving. Team Good was having a party. Good for them. It was time for her to go back to a very different party and deliver bad news that the main entertainment had fled.

The mood was incredibly festive at Mother Goose's cottage. Everyone was there in their most bright and cheerful outfits. Flamboyant rainbows of color danced around the house at every corner. Even the Grimm brothers had been given festive clothing to wear, finer than any they had ever known. It was hard to believe that mere hours ago, they were at the terrifying castle of Queen Gretel.

When they had first arrived, the house had been very quiet. This was because Daisy had sent everyone away to get refreshed and ready for the evening's festivities. They had all returned now and it was brilliant. Everywhere they turned, there were fairies, magical creatures, witches, magicians, elves, sprites, even brownies, and one disgruntled leprechaun. Nowhere did they find Rumpelstiltskin though.

Every person who showed up also brought a beautifully wrapped gift that they left on a table in the parlor. The parlor itself seemed to have tripled in size from when they had first arrived. Clearly, there was some form of magic responsible for this. This was unimportant at the moment. Now they would spend the evening meeting and talking to as many of these amazing creatures as they could, learning their stories and tales. Both boys were ecstatic at the new stories they would be able to collect just on this night and record in their magic journal.

The party was great fun. Daisy and Basil even looked light-hearted, like they hadn't a care in the world. After the food had been eaten, the dancing began. Music streamed into the room seemingly from invisible musicians. Wilhelm found himself wondering if ghosts existed, and if so, were they playing the music? Did this mean that they were friendly or merely servants? As he began to look for a witch or wizard that he could ask the question of ghosts to, the music stopped and Daisy spoke over the crowd.

"Attention, everyone. We are going to have a brief break from dancing." An exasperated gasp rose among the crowd. "Don't fret, we will get back to dancing shortly. But first, it's time for presents!" A cheer went up around the room.

Jacob and Wilhelm looked at each other with worry. They had not brought gifts for anyone. It is not as if they had had time to plan being here at all. As if he sensed their concern, Basil showed up right on cue.

"You look troubled, my boys," he said kindly.

"It's just that we didn't know we needed to bring gifts," said Wilhelm.

"Not to worry. Daisy has taken care of that. There are two extra ones already out there so that you two may participate in the fun as well. It is a new sort of game we are going to play. We draw lots to see in what order we pick the gifts, and then take turns choosing a gift and opening it. If the next person likes your gift, they can forgo opening the one they pick in lieu of taking yours and giving you the one that they have chosen. It should be a fun time."

It sounded a little convoluted to the boys, but who were they to turn away a free gift for no apparent reason? The first few rounds were entertaining to watch as people playfully argued over stolen gifts. So far, the prized gift had been a beautiful crystal that was deep purple with many facets and emanated its own light. It pulsed gently in a mesmerizing rhythm.

Jacob ended up with a lovely new quill that had been given by a griffin from his own feathers. Wilhelm had received a rock. As best he could tell, it was just a plain gray rock. He was a little disappointed, hoping to receive an amazing and magical gift, but hid it well and boasted about it being one of the prettiest and most well-shaped stones he had seen. The wood nymph that had picked it had been standing next to him when he made his statements of appreciation, and she beamed with pride over her amazing abilities to give gifts to complete strangers. She then proceeded to tell him the entire tale of her search for the perfect stone, recounting the numerous other stones that she had chosen to reject.

Now it was Daisy's turn to choose a gift. Not feeling right about stealing something from another person, even though she had invented the game and the rules, she chose a box and opened it immediately. She dropped to the ground in horror, her mouth open in a silent scream. Basil waddled over as quickly as he could to see what had shocked her so.

He peered in and let out a gasp. It was Luna's head. There was also a note in the box. Jacob, having been somewhat desensitized to gruesome acts like this from his time with Gretel, reached into the box, pulled out the note, and read it aloud.

Dearest Mother Goose and friends,

You have made it clear that we are enemies and you will feel no remorse disposing of poor, innocent children like us. And so we will extend the same terms to you: no remorse and no mercy. This is now a war, officially. If you send any more of yours to us, they too will be returned in boxes. As a matter of fact, we may get a head start on that. Why wait for you to make a move? I will be in touch soon.

Best wishes,
"Gretel of the Children's Rebellion"

Basil broke the silence that followed.

"Jacob, could I trouble you to please remove this?" Jacob picked up the box and left the room. "This is indeed a sad event. Luna was well loved and well liked. She had done her job and was retired. She was so brave and came back to us in our time of need. We will never be able to repay her for this gift she has given to us. It is a great loss but we will recover. I am sorry, but I think it is time for this party to be over and everyone to return home for an evening of quiet reflection and grieving in each of our own ways. Thank you all for being here. Be safe and travel home as quickly as you can. Remember to have your amulets on at all times. Good night, everyone."

Jacob and Wilhelm returned to their room as soon as the guests had left so Basil and Daisy could mourn privately.

"Things have really gotten bad haven't they?" asked Wilhelm.

"These are dark days. It is sad. That poor old lady. I feel bad that this was also one of the best nights of my life. Should I feel guilty that I am still excited about everything till that point?"

"We didn't know her and we have seen much worse over the last few months. I think we should hold on to every bit of happiness that we can. We are going to learn magic!"

"How did you become so wise, little brother?"
"No idea."

"Do you want to record some of the stories that we heard tonight?" Jacob asked excitedly.

"Of course I do! I have been waiting to do that all night. Where do you want to start?"

The brothers stayed up until the wee hours of the morning, recounting the various stories they had heard so that their magic journal could record all of the details for them. Meanwhile, Daisy and Basil were up till the wee hours, recording their memories in tears spilled into teacups.

Gretel was unhappy when she heard the news about the Grimm brothers running away, but was not overly surprised. They seemed weak and did not serve much purpose other than being record keepers and entertainers. They certainly were failures in the spy department. That odd party that Mother Goose had thrown was the most useful information that she had managed to extract from them. They would be no great loss. But still, it did reflect poorly on her leadership to have people escape unharmed. She did not feel like chasing them, though. Maybe she could use some of the leftover bodies from their next raid and convince people that they were the brothers. Yes, that is what she would do. Fortunately, their next raid was tonight. Snow had stumbled upon a fairy glen while she was out recruiting. Fairies were not much for fighting and these were minor fairies, not like the fairy godmother or that pesky blue fairy. These were small in stature and had little in the way of magic. They would be easy to trap. And being the size of children instead of full grown adults, she could surely pass off two of them as the Grimms without a problem. Just rip their little wings off and give them a good even charring. No one would know. Kill two birds with one stone, as they say.

Later that evening, they loaded up a large number of cages onto a few wagons and headed towards the fairy glen. Gretel was staying home for this one but gave Snow very strict instructions to keep an eye out for anything magical. Frequently, the fairies hide magical treasures in tree stumps or hollowed out logs.

When the troop returned, they were all accounted for and all in good spirits. Gretel pulled Rose aside.

"Do you see those two fairies there? I have a special task for you and you alone. You must tell no one, not even your sister, of this. Not even Red or Hansel. This is between us and I think this will bond us closer as friends and allies. This is your chance at redemption."

Rose shook her head vigorously to signal that she grasped the severity of the request, and also that she was ready to be redeemed in Gretel's eyes. She felt sure that if she could do this task, whatever it was, and keep this secret, her position would once again be secured.

"Good," said Gretel. "I need you to take those two fairies, remove their wings completely and any other distinguishing characteristic that marks them as fairies. Then I want you to char their flesh so they are unrecognizable but still maintain their basic forms. We are going to make these the Grimm brothers. The underlings must not think it is okay to walk in and out of this army as they please. They must know that deserters will not be tolerated. Do you understand?"

"I do. I will make them very convincing, Gretel. You can count on me."

"I hope I can."

Rose left to make space for all of the prisoners and to prepare for the craft project of making fairies into burned boys.

Snow rushed to Gretel when she was finished speaking with her sister.

"I found something that I think might interest you very much." Snow pulled a wooden box out from behind her back and presented it to Gretel. Gretel turned it over in her hands and considered it thoughtfully.

"Do you know what it is or what it does?"

"Oh yes and I think you will like it very much. It is a puzzle box. When you open it, it creates an underground labyrinth, a deadly one that no one has ever survived. The person who opens it becomes a hideous beast the fairies called a Minotaur and is forced to hunt and murder those who enter. He is eternally imprisoned until someone kills him and defeats the maze. In the center of the maze is a golden treasure that will return you to the outside. The fairy said that no one has escaped it before. The Minotaur is not the only deadly thing in the labyrinth, though. There are traps as well as other monsters and angry ghosts of past victims. The Fairy Godmother somehow hid the labyrinth in this box so that wayward travelers would stop stumbling into it."

"Interesting, indeed. This is fantastic. Well done, Snow," Gretel said, and gave her a quick hug. Things were looking up.

The next morning, Gretel assembled the whole army behind the castle.

"We are adding an expansion onto our home and I wanted everyone to see it. Even those we thought we had lost will get to be present. Rose, please escort our friends Jacob and Wilhelm Grimm out here, if you will."

Red's throat tightened. What was going on? How could they have gotten them from Mother Goose? How did she not know about it? Did Gretel suspect her? Was Jacob alright? At that moment, Rose and Hansel wheeled out a cage that had two charred remains inside. Acid and tears rose in Red's throat. Her eyes stung as she bit back the burning hot tears desperately trying to free themselves.

"They were found on the road not far from here during our victory feast when we dealt with our other little betrayer. As a matter of fact, let's bring him out as well. He should be here to see this too."

Red took a deep breath. That could not be Jacob. She had talked to Mother Goose during that feast, and Jacob and Wilhelm were at the party with her . . . or was she lying? Right now, Red would have to cling to the belief that Mother Goose was being truthful, and Gretel was the one spewing falsehoods, which was far more likely. Still, it puzzled and troubled her that she had not been included in the ruse.

Rose and Hansel wheeled out another cage, this one with a very lively and animated Prince inside. He was dirty, disheveled, and clearly aware of his appearance.

"Charming, so good of you to join us. We thought as part of our little family, you should be included in the grand reveal of our new expansion. As a matter of fact, I would like you to do the honors." She leaned towards his cage and spoke in words soft enough for only him to hear. "If you want to be back on my good side, make a good show of this. Prove that you are one of us, I shall release you from this cage, and you will never have to go back to that dungeon again."

"You swear it?"

"I do."

She turned back to the crowd. "In a sign of good faith, our resident noble Prince Charming has rather magnanimously agreed to do the honors of opening the new section for us."

She handed him the box and opened the cage. He stepped out onto the grass, smiled his most dazzling smile to the crowd, and gave a little wave. Gretel showed him which pieces of the box to move, and when he had, she had him place the box on the ground and take a few steps back. The ground began to shake and moan. Then it began to grow into the shape of a small dome with a doorway and a very ornate gate closing the front of it off. After many minutes had passed, the ground became stationary once more and silence filled the air. Everyone began clapping and cheering. "Where does it lead?" came shouts from the crowd. Gretel waited to respond to them for she knew that the show was not yet over. A moment later, Charming let out a howl of pain and dropped to the ground, clutching his stomach.

"What is happening? What have you done to me?"

"Nothing you don't deserve, my prince. Nothing you don't deserve."

The crowd watched in shock as Charming's body twisted and contorted, bones breaking and skin tearing, all the while his screams of agony growing louder and deeper. Fur and horns forced their way through his head and body. When it was all over, he slowly stood. He was at least 9 feet tall, not including the massive horns protruding from his head. He had hooves and red eyes. He looked part man and part bull.

Gretel signaled Rose to bring the draped mirror that had been standing off to the side over to the beast that had been Prince Charming. She pulled the fabric aside. Charming stared in horror at the reflection. He was hideous, a monster in every way. How would he ever show himself in public again? No one would be with him ever again. It was too much for him, and he turned away from the horrific visage reflected in the mirror.

He turned on Gretel. She would pay for this. All of this was her fault. He bared down on her and as he was about to charge, the gate swung open behind him, drawing his attention. He was drawn to it. He knew that he should resist, that if he went into the doorway, he would never come out again, and never get his revenge on Gretel. Yet he could not resist its pull. Though he struggled against it, he walked into the opening, and the gate slammed shut behind him. As soon as it did, the pull vanished and the weight of what had happened crashed in on him. He would never feel the sun on his skin again. He opened his mouth to curse Gretel for what she had done, to tell everyone of the injustices he had suffered, but the only sound that came out was an indistinguishable roar. Not only had he lost his freedom, his body, his life, he had also lost his powers of speech. He was now just a monster, a wild animal in a cage for eternity. After one last look at his past comrades, he walked down the stairs to become acquainted with his new home.

Gretel smiled to herself. She had managed to make one thing very clear with two distinct messages. Never betray her trust. Today was going exactly as she had hoped. She caught a quick glance of Red as she turned. As she suspected, Red was staring not at the labyrinth but at the charred remains in the cage. Likely she was mourning the loss of her beloved Jacob. Gretel supposed that she should feel bad for her friend and her loss, but in truth, she was downright gleeful. Red was hers and hers alone once again, with no distractions and no hope that he would return to her at some point. That was why she had not been included in that little plot with Rose. If Red thought Jacob was dead, she would stop looking for him.

"This," Gretel said, motioning to the gate, "is the labyrinth. It is a giant maze full of danger and death. You go in; you don't come out again. No one knows the horrors that await inside because no one has come out to tell of them. I would recommend that you all stay far away from this gate. We wouldn't want any of you getting sucked in accidentally. Now I am off to have a chat with Mother Goose. The rest of you, have an excellent day."

Gretel headed back to her cottage with Red trailing behind. Red would check with Mother Goose later in private. She would demand to see Jacob and know that he was safe before Red gave her any more information, and she had a lot of information for

Mother Goose this time. In the meantime, she would have to make a show of being at least a little distraught over the reveal of the impostor body of the boy that Gretel clearly knew she cared for.

When they had arrived at the cottage, Gretel settled herself down in front of the crystal ball and got comfortable. Red positioned herself behind Gretel so that she could see Mother Goose and vice versa.

"Mother Goose," called Gretel and waited. After a few moments, the ball glowed and Daisy appeared. She looked horrible. She clearly had not slept. "I see you must have gotten my gift. I hope you liked it."

"How dare you speak to me this way? You are pure evil."

"Be that as it may, I have a deal to offer you. I have a whole dungeon full of fairy friends of yours. I also have a castle full of psychopaths and a shining new labyrinth with a fresh, angry Minotaur. Those friends of yours are in for a very hard and long week if you don't surrender the locations of all of your operatives to me. I will torture and kill every last one of these innocent fairies. They never worked for you or hunted for you or killed for you, but they will pay the price if you don't give me all of the records on your operatives. I already know who there are, just not where. You have one hour to consider this offer; then, we throw the first fairy in the labyrinth and the second one on a spit for dinner. I will make sure to bring the crystal ball with me so that you can hear every last tormented scream that issues from them as they slowly die for your decision. I await your response." Gretel waved her wand at the crystal and it went dark.

She spun around and faced Red. "I assume you have some choice words for me."

"Why did you have to kill him? You told them to run away in the night if they did not belong here, and that is what they did," said Red plainly.

"Because a lesson had to be taught. I know you are mad now, but in time that will fade, and you will see that I am right about this. Why don't you take the rest of the day off to clear your head?"

"I should be here for Mother Goose's response," said Red, trying to sound like her old, friendly self.

"Ah, throw yourself into your work. I see. Good idea actually. Nothing helps heartache like causing heartache in others and watching dreams collapse. Plus, I would hate for you to miss one of the most important moments in history: the moment Mother Goose surrendered to me."

After about 45 minutes, the crystal ball flared into life. "Gretel? Come here this instant, you wretched child," said Daisy.

"Well, early. I like that. You goodie-goodies can never resist saving lives of the innocent. How will you be sending me the information I've requested?"

"I will not be sending you anything. I am merely giving you the chance to reconsider. You do not have to do this. Perhaps instead, we could set you and your brother up on your own island, away from the reach of anyone else. You could live out your lives there in comfort. We would monitor you closely so that no others were harmed, but you yourself would be left to your own devices as long as you stayed out of trouble and on that island. That is my offer to you."

"No. Are you really devaluing the lives of the innocent ones that I have here over the murderers that you employ? I am surprised and a little impressed. I did not believe you would be able to be that cold and heartless. Well done. I win no matter what you decide in this situation. Are you sure that your final decision is to withhold the information that I asked for?"

"You will not have the information," Daisy said tersely. "But I also will not watch them perish."

"Oh, won't you? Will you really let their lives mean so little that you don't even pay them the respect of watching them suffer and die for your choices? If you were a truly good person, you would witness their sacrifices. The choice is yours."

Gretel picked up the heavy crystal ball and carried it with her to the dungeon.

"Rose!" she commanded, "You are to begin executing the captors. Make it slow and make sure that you do it in front of this crystal ball. You may or may not have an audience from time to time. Put on a good show for them. I expect that this will be a job that takes at least a week. Also, throw one of them a day into the labyrinth to keep our noble Minotaur happy and fed."

"Of course, Gretel. They shall all have the pleasure of unique, entertaining, and excruciating deaths. This is a great time for your brother to join me as well if he is interested. There are quite a few of them, so I could use the help."

"I will send word to him. I am sure he will be delighted by the invitation." Gretel left Rose to her work.

Chapter 6

"Now what, Basil? I assume you have a plan, a way to free them, a rescue mission. What do we do? Who do we call?" Daisy asked confident Basil would never allow innocents to be lost.

"There is no plan," the goose said morosely. "We must let them die. We will not give Gretel the satisfaction of watching the torture, though."

"What?! You can't be serious. We have to help them."

"We can't, Daisy. It is too late for them. I am sorry, but sometimes hard choices have to be made."

Just then, there was a knock at the door. Daisy, happy to leave the room that Basil was occupying, practically jumped at the opportunity to answer it. She flung the door open wide and gasped in astonishment. On the other side stood Maleficent, proud and foreboding as ever.

"Maleficent! What are you doing here? I thought you had left us for good," stammered Daisy.

"Shall I stand out here all night or will you ask me to come in?" Maleficent asked, unmoved by Daisy's rudeness and shock.

"Of course, I am so sorry! Where are my manners? We have had quite an evening thus

far and my mind is all a-tizzy." Maleficent continued to stand in the doorway but arched a stoic eyebrow and nodded her head.

"Oh!" cried Daisy as she leaped out of the entry way so that Maleficent could pass. "I'm so sorry. Would you like to adjourn to the parlor?"

Maleficent glided into the parlor and took a seat. Basil was already there and looked quite flabbergasted to see his former coworker enter the room.

"Good day, Basil. You are looking . . . fat and old if I am being honest."

"And you look as severe as ever," Basil replied, calmly.

"Thank you. Now to the reason I am here. It seems as though you have grown up a little, accepted that some things cannot be changed, and some people cannot be saved. You have to make some sacrifices for the greater good. That means that you are finally being honest with yourselves, and I can work with that. I am here to offer my services in the coming war against the so-called Children's Rebellion. Daisy, don't you normally offer a guest tea?"

Daisy had always been intimidated by Maleficent and took the opportunity to leave the room and the oppressive atmosphere.

"I take it that you were watching through the crystal ball then?' asked Basil.

"I was. It was exactly the kind of growth I was looking for from you. Sometimes you need to be a monster to defeat one."

"I would not call that being a monster, Maleficent."

"If I had done it instead of you, you would have called me a monster, Basil. Would you like to retain my services again or not?"

"Yes, we need someone like you."

"Monster at your service, Basil. Now, I assume you would like to attempt a rescue of the ones that you can correct? She won't be expecting it."

"I had not gotten that far yet, but ideally, yes."

Daisy entered with a tray of tea. "I thought you just said that they were all lost to us now and we would not be saving them?"

"I was trying to avoid getting your hopes up, dear. I had not formed a plan yet. But I think I have one now. We need to talk to the Troll King. I think they might enjoy a little raid," Basil said with a twinkle in his eye.

"Trolls? Why not send someone stealthier and . . . well, smarter instead?" asked Maleficent.

"Because I think a show of force and strength is more appropriate this time. We showed them that we can make the hard choices and lose a battle to win the war; now it's time to show them that we can win the battles, too."

"Really, Daisy, you do make a fine cup of tea." sneered Maleficent.

Bartholomew the Troll King was happy enough to receive the message for Mother Goose. He was to take a raiding party of trolls to Gretel's castle, bash some heads, and free some fairies. He had not always been aligned with Mother Goose and the cause of the greater good. He and his brethren used to spend their time under bridges snacking on wayward children. Then one day, the Fairy Godmother had shown up and stolen a tasty little morsel of a girl from him. He still remembered her fat little cheeks. He was furious, but Godmother had far more power and strength than he had, and she trapped him in a magical cage. Many days passed, and he wondered why she did not kill him and be done with it. Why was she keeping him in a cage? She brought him food and water. She also brought him books to pass his time in confinement. He was not much of a reader, though; so she talked to him instead. They had long wonderful talks about interests, history, and family. Through their talks, she had learned that shoe making was a hobby of his, so she brought him leather and tools to use for cobbling.

Weeks passed this way and they became friends. One day, she asked him if she were to let him go, would he attack her again? He told her that he would not and she knew this to be true. Then she asked him if he would continue to eat children. He told her that he would, as it was his nature, and she knew that also to be true. She left him then for a full day's time. During that time, he made the most wondrous shoes he had ever made. They were beautiful. When the Godmother returned, she remarked on their beauty and asked if she might add a little magic to them herself. He was very excited by the honor of it and quickly agreed. She touched her wand to them and they became glass. Somehow, they were even more beautiful than before. She told him that these shoes had the gift to transform whoever wore them into whomever they wanted to be. She passed them back to Bartholomew since they were his masterpieces, but he pushed them away. He told her that he had made them for her as a gift for her kindness and friendship. She thanked him and graciously accepted the shoes.

That was not the end of what she had to talk to him about that day, however. She had left him to speak with Mother Goose herself and ask for approval of him becoming a part of their community. The Troll

King was very confused, as he had been honest about continuing to eat children.

The Fairy Godmother explained to him about the dark ones, and that the Troll King would be sent on missions to kill or eat as many of them as he wanted, as long as he could promise not to eat any other children. If he could make this pledge to her, he would have his freedom. He was overjoyed by this and quickly vowed to only eat children who were classified as dark ones.

He was distraught when he heard the news of the Fairy Godmother's death. He loved her dearly. He knew he would never love another again the way that he had loved her. Since that day, he had felt a darkness growing inside of him.

He and his band of trolls arrived at the castle in good time and stopped at the gate.

"I WILL SPEAK TO THE ONE IN CHARGE HERE!" his voice boomed up to the ramparts. Within minutes, a blonde girl appeared on the wall.

"What do you want, mighty Troll King?" she replied.

"I want to eat every last one of you. Let me in." Trolls were not known for their intelligence, and he had not been given any ideas on how to get into the castle. Bartholomew decided he would try the easiest approach first and just ask.

"Oh, well then. I think I am going to have to deny you entry. I prefer not to be eaten, but thank you for your inquiry," replied Gretel.

"Now I will just have to find another way in. Why couldn't you have just made this easy?"

"Might I ask why you are here to eat us all?"

"Mother Goose sent us," he replied, a little annoyed.

"Oh, I was under the impression that a king answered to no one, especially an old woman with a goose and no real title."

Bartholomew took a moment to think about that. He was a king. Why was he taking his orders from some old lady? What did he get out of this deal anyway? The Godmother was gone, so he was not doing it for her anymore. And he was not let loose to eat children nearly as often as he was told he would be. Most of the dark ones he was allowed to eat were all in this castle anyway, where he couldn't get to them.

"Why aren't you going after children who aren't locked away in a castle? Surely that would be a better plan?" asked Gretel.

"Well, dark ones are the only children we are allowed to eat these days."

"Is it some kind of diet? You look pretty skinny to me like you haven't had a hearty meal in years. All of this shouting back and forth is starting to hurt my throat. Tell you what. If I bring you a child to eat, do you promise not to eat me if I come out there to talk with you?"

"Why would you sacrifice one of your army to talk to me?"

"Oh, don't be silly, it won't be one of mine. I could bring you one of the local village children, fresh from the farm. But you must swear not to eat me."

He thought about it for a time. It would mean breaking his promise to the Godmother, but she was dead anyway. Plus, who would know if he had one little snack that was off the menu?

"Fine, I swear on my finest boots, I will not eat you."

"Or maim or kill me in any way."

"Or maim or kill you in any way," he dutifully repeated.

"Excellent!"

Gretel went out of the castle alone, as she had only negotiated her own safety thus far. Plus, she had the Godmother's wand with her. She felt quite safe and sure of herself.

"Where is my snack?" asked the Troll King.

"I will bring her out after we have had a chat," said Gretel. Bartholomew was secretly happy to hear that it was a girl. He hoped she had fat cheeks. "Now," continued Gretel, "it seems that you have orders from Mother Goose to come and eat us all. I can't let that happen. What I can do is strike a deal with you."

"What kind of deal?"

"Well, there are only so many of us dark ones. You would run out very quickly once you got inside. But there are a lot of regular children. If I have my story correct and I think I do, you used to eat normal children as often as you would like. Why the change in diet to only dark ones? And why would you take orders from Mother Goose? You are far more powerful than she is, especially with the band of trolls you command."

"I made a deal with the Fairy Godmother long ago that I would only kill dark ones."

"And she is dead. You made no deal with Mother Goose. She has no power over you. Join us instead. For every town we take, we will make sure to save the fattest child for you. When the final battle comes, I want you to fight with us instead. Then, when we win, you may roam the countryside eating and killing whomever you like, as long as they do not reside in my castle or are under my protection. Don't worry; the under-my-protection list is very small. What do you say? You would have your freedom back again, and all you have to do is what comes naturally to you and help me in one little battle. Do we have a deal?"

Bartholomew thought about it for a minute and could see no faults in this plan. He had no one to impress anymore.

"We have a deal. Now, where is my snack?"

Gretel walked back into the castle and then returned with the chubby girl from the town led by a rope. She passed the end of the rope to Bartholomew and walked back into the castle without a second glance.

Jacob and Wilhelm had decided to keep to themselves for a while following the party. Things had gotten very tense in the cottage after that, with good reason. Wilhelm spent most of his time with the white rabbit trying to catch up on entries, while Jacob directed his time to research. He poured over files for hours at a time, taking notes and cross-referencing anything that seemed like it may have been a connection between stories of verified dark ones. It was a lot of information to sort through, but in a very short amount of time, he felt confident he had a lead.

There seemed to be a common thread between a few of the stories. Rapunzel, Hansel and Gretel, Cinderella . . . their mothers all had a craving for rampion. On its own, this was not a big discovery.

Rampion was fairly common and many people enjoyed its flavor. But looking deeper, the description many gave of what they ate was not exactly rampion, but something that looked similar. A past agent of Mother Goose's found it interesting enough to note and make a sketch of the plant, but no one seemed to have looked any deeper into the matter. Now he just had to figure out what to do with this information. Rapunzel's file included a location of where her father had found the plant. It was in the garden of a witch, which seemed odd to him since as far as he knew, all of the witches were working with Daisy and Basil.

"Mr. Hare? Who is the witch that is referred to in this file? Is it someone that we work with?"

"Oh no, Jacob. That is not one of our witches," said the rabbit.

"So there are bad witches as well as good ones? I thought they all worked with Daisy."

"No, there have been some dark ones in the past who have slipped through the cracks. We can't get them all. And at some point, they grow up. Many of them became witches or sorcerers."

"Do you know the one this file is talking about? Is she still alive?"

"Oh, she is still alive, for sure and certain. Her name is Hecuba. Nasty sort she is but she tends to keep to herself and her garden. As long as you stay out of her garden, you are safe, which is why we have not wasted resources hunting her down. We do keep an eye on her though, making sure she stays out of trouble."

"So no one ever checked to see what she is growing there?"

"Well, we are kind of busy trying to save the world all the time, you know. If there is one witch who just tends to her garden and only smites people who trespass and steal from her, I think we are doing alright!"

Jacob let it rest, sensing that he would get nowhere talking to the March hare. He did not believe that Basil or Daisy were in any position to help him out either right now. He would have to do this on his own then. That was fine by him. Now that he knew who she was, it should be easy enough to find out where she was.

Jacob told his brother his plan to go find the witch Hecuba and ask her questions directly about her garden. Wilhelm was leery of this plan and tried to persuade his brother to talk to Basil instead. Jacob would hear none of it, insisting that he had to do this because the others were too busy with more important matters. He went to the room that they shared and began packing a small bag with food for his trip. It would take him the better part of a day to get there and back again, but he should be home before anyone took notice that he was missing. It would have been much faster for one of the magical beings to do this, but he would have to make do with his own two mortal, non-magical feet.

As he placed the last of his supplies into his sack, there was a knock at the door, followed immediately by the entrance of Daisy and Basil. He dropped the bag onto the bed, hoping it did not arouse suspicion.

"Jacob, there is someone who would like to speak with you," Daisy said, and help up the small mirror that matched the one he had been given and had in turn given to Red. Red's face showed through the reflection.

"Red! Are you well? Is everything alright?" Jacob exclaimed with a mixture of excitement and concern.

"I am fine, everything is fine...well, actually I suppose everything is fairly awful all around but I personally am safe and unharmed. I wanted to see with my own eyes that you did indeed make it to Mother Goose. And your brother is with you as well?"

"Yes, he is. He is working; did you want me to get him?"

"No, I don't have time for that. I just needed to see you. Gretel had burned bodies that she claimed were you and your brother. I could not be sure until now that you were safe. I have to go now, but please thank Mother Goose for me." And the mirror went back to being a mirror and all he saw was his own face, reflecting a cross between joy from seeing the girl he loved and sadness that she was now gone.

"Going somewhere?" asked Basil, eyeing the bag on the bed.

"Oh, I uh, thought I might go for a bit of a walk . . ."

"To visit a certain garden perhaps? Wilhelm told us. Don't be mad at him. That is what you should have told us from the start. You must never lie or keep secrets if you are going to stay here. I know that is what you had to do to survive at the castle, and perhaps it was wrong of us to put you in that position in the first place, but that is over now."

"I'm sorry. I just know that you are all so busy with such important things. I didn't think you would have time for something like this."

"This is an important thing as well. This could be the information that we need to finally know who is and isn't a dark one. It could take all of the guesswork out of it. But we would not know that if you had gone off on your own and gotten yourself killed or hurt, would we? Now, we need to figure out who to send to talk with Hecuba . . . someone she can relate to . . . maybe someone who could be her friend . . . Of course! Daisy, get Maleficent back here, please."

"What is that?" Gretel asked from the doorway of Red's room. Red spun around with the small mirror in her hand. Gretel had only been to her room once. Generally, she sent other people to fetch her when she was needed.

"Woah, you completely startled me, Gret," Red said, to cover her nervousness. "You never come up here. Is something wrong?"

"Nothing is wrong; just thought I might see what you do when you are not with me," Gretel said as she walked closer to Red. She reached out and took the mirror from her and turned it around in her hands, examining it closer.

"It's a trinket I took off Charming when we locked him up. No big surprise he carried a mirror with him. I didn't think you would appreciate him being able to check his hair while he was locked away. It's pretty, so I figured I would keep it for myself."

"And so you could make sure you were presentable for that Grimm boy, of course." Gretel threw the mirror back to Red and upon catching it,

Red pocketed it immediately so that it would be out of sight and out of mind. "That is actually why I came up. I wanted to chat with you, but in a place where you are comfortable."

"Well, we should be doing it at your cottage then, because I spend far more time there than I do here. And when I am here, I am generally asleep." Red sat on the bed and Gretel did the same.

"What were you doing while I was attacking the village the other day? The day the Grimm's fled."

"I was snooping through people's rooms, seeing if I could find anything interesting or condemning."

"And did you? What did you find when you looked through Jacob and Wilhelm's room?"

"Their journal, which surprised me, because I assumed that they always had it with them. I looked through it and it seemed to actually just be a bunch of stories. Many of them were the ones they told after dinner. I think they were probably just boys looking for adventure, and then they got scared when they realized they were out of their league. I guess we will never know now. Did you find their book on them when you caught them?"

"What did you talk about when you last saw Jacob?" Gretel pushed. It was becoming clear to Red that this was not a friendly chat, and was, in fact, an interrogation. For some reason, Gretel was suspicious of her now. She would have to be very careful with her answers.

"He kissed me." The safest thing was to keep it as close to the truth as possible.

"He kissed you!?" Real shock registered in Gretel's face and voice. "What did he say and why didn't you tell me?"

"He said he liked me and he wanted to know more about me. I told him that there was not much to tell that he didn't already know and that I didn't want to show up in one of his stories, then he kissed me and ran off. That was the last time I saw him. It's probably for the best; it never would have worked out anyway. I don't have time for naive people in my life. As for why I didn't tell you, you may not have noticed, but you are a little busy with planning a war and studying magic as fast as you can. A kiss from a boy is hardly newsworthy compared to that."

"You are my sister, the person I am closest to in this world. Of course I want to hear about your life. Now that I know all of this, I suspect the reason he fled was more from rejection than fear. His brother was probably fear; the younger ones are always the weaker ones when it comes to siblings." Gretel sighed. Red made a mental note of this sentiment. It was clear that she was referring not only to Wilhelm but also to her own brother Hansel. "Also, I am sorry that I had to kill him. It was for the best and I wouldn't change what I did. I am sorry that it may have hurt or affected you in some way, though."

"Don't worry about me, Gret. I am fine. It was a shock to see their charred bodies of course, but mostly I was shocked and hurt because you did not tell me about it," Red lied.

"I had to be sure that you were on my side above everyone else."

"You know that I am. I owe you my life. You saved me."

Gretel leaned over and embraced Red. There was still something tugging at her mind, telling her not to trust Red completely. But that would be for another day. For now, she had her friend back and that was all that mattered; she had her sister with whom she could share her victories and burdens.

"So," Gretel released her and continued in a more conspiratorial tone, "was he a good kisser?"

They both giggled; Gretel, genuine laughter, and Red, a laugh to cover her disdain and sadness.

"Well, it's nice to see you in a good mood for a change," said Red, to change the subject.

"And why shouldn't I be in a good mood? I have trolls now!" Gretel said with a childlike glee.

This was bad and all Red could think about was getting a message to Mother Goose, partly because it would be important information for them to have, and if she was being completely honest, which she rarely was these days, partially to possibly catch a glimpse of Jacob in the background. Their conversation had not been long enough, or private enough, for that matter. She found herself daydreaming about him stealing the mirror from Mother Goose's pocket somehow, and using it to call to her to profess his undying love and beg her once more to come away with him.

"Red. Red?" Gretel said. "Are you alright?"

Oh no, she had been daydreaming instead of paying attention. This had never happened to Red before and it was a dangerous thing. She would have to be aware of that in the future and be much more cautious. "I'm fine. I'm sorry. I haven't been getting very much sleep lately. But trolls, yay. That's great news."

Maleficent had insisted on going to Hecuba's on her own. They wanted information from this dark witch and the only way Maleficent was going to get it was by convincing Hecuba that she was on her side. There is no way that could have happened with some shining beacon of white light by her side. Honestly, what did they think they were going to do to get the information out of her? Tickle fight, probably. This was better. She would approach her as an ally, someone who parted ways with Mother Goose because of irreconcilable differences. Fortunately, she had taken her leave of Mother Goose and company in a big way and rumors of it had spread quickly. When Maleficent had returned, however, it was in the dark of night and in hushed tones. The only ones who knew what side she was on for sure right now were Basil and Daisy. She had a great advantage in this and would use it as much as she could.

Maleficent glided to the door of the shack in the woods, for that is all that it was: a dumpy, falling-down shack that looked as if it were held together with prayers and spit. The fence that encircled the back of the house was a different story entirely. It was less of a fence and more a stone wall, six feet high with no gate. She imagined the only way in was through the hovel or using a ladder to climb over the wall.

Maleficent had done a little research before heading off to pay a call to Hecuba. Hecuba had been a dark one as a child. She slipped through the cracks because she never did anything overt to anyone. She mainly kept to her garden, and as a result, she was deemed a low priority. This may have been a mistake. Unfortunately, there was not much for Maleficent to go on in the rather thin record they had on her. She was orphaned at a young age. She still resided in her childhood home in the woods. Her mother had been a witch as well, but it seemed she had not been a dark one herself. The mother Herminia had worked with the previous Mother Goose. Daisy was, of course, not the first with that title. No one knew if Basil was the goose of the previous Mother or not. Maleficent herself suspected that he was indeed. She had a theory that he was the original Goose and just changed "Mothers" when one got old and died. The Mothers never showed any outward signs of power or magic themselves.

Herminia was the keeper of the garden of good. Just as there were good and evil humans, magical beings, animals, and even places, so too were there good and evil plants. Evil plants may sound unrealistic to most, but try to get a child to eat broccoli and you will see the truth of it. It was rumored that the garden of good had contained miraculous plants, and the most well-known of these was the Tree of Life. It was a golden tree that produced sweet fruit that could heal wounds instantly and extend youth and beauty. When Herminia passed away, the garden suddenly fell into disrepair and the plants she protected all withered away. Many suspected the little daughter of poisoning Herminia, but no one did an in-depth investigation. They did not have many of the resources then that they had now in handling these matters, so much was left undocumented.

Maleficent raised her hand to knock on the door and hesitated. She worried that a slight breeze would be enough to collapse the shack. A solid knock would likely make the entire door crumble away. Her hand hung in midair balled into a fist while she debated the merits of knocking versus speaking loudly to get Hecuba's attention. That is when the door swung open to reveal a shriveled old woman, stooped and feeble. She looked like the living embodiment of the shack that was her dwelling.

"Who are you and what do you want?" the thin frail voice demanded abruptly.

"Are you Hecuba?" asked Maleficent as she gracefully lowered her hand.

"I asked you first, lady," snarled the small woman.

"I am Maleficent and I want to speak with you about your garden." Maleficent's voice was smooth, rich, and cool, the opposite of Hecuba's in every way.

"Maleficent? Aren't you the one who abandoned Mother Goose? Oh, don't look so surprised. I may be a hermit but I have my ways of keeping up with the latest gossip. What do you want with my garden?"

"You still have not answered my question. Are you Hecuba?"

"Yes, of course I am. Who else would I be? I thought you were supposed to be clever. Now, what do you want with my garden?"

"Revenge, of course."

"Come right in, then," Hecuba opened the door and stepped to the side, leaving room for Maleficent to walk through. Maleficent had to duck to enter and once she was inside, she was shocked by the squalor. It was somehow even worse than it had been outside. Apparently, Herminia died before teaching her daughter how to keep a house, even a small one such as this, in working order. There was a stench that permeated every inch of the place, and as she looked around, she could see it came from rotting food and trash left in corners, and in fact, on every available surface. It took all of her concentration to keep her face blank and her breakfast in place.

Hecuba pointed toward a rickety wooden chair covered in shredded fabric and bits of refuse. "Have a seat and tell me what you are looking for."

Maleficent stared in disgust at the spindly seat. "I enjoy standing, thank you."

"Sit or leave. You are in my home and will obey my rules if you want something from me."

Maleficent, using two fingers, upset the chair enough for the debris to fall away. She chose to ignore the stains, instead of questioning where they came from.

"I want to make Mother Goose and her friends hurt. They have never trusted me or liked me, and I am tired of their arrogance. I have heard rumors that you have a plant. It looks similar to rampion but is not the same at all. It is rumored that this plant has the power to create dark ones from normal people. My hope is that it can also make dark ones out of magical people."

"Interesting. I do indeed possess such a plant. I call it Herminia after my mother. It will unfortunately not work on those who are truly good and pure of heart. It will only work when there is already a seed of evil in them. It nurtures and brings those tendencies to the surface."

"How do you know it will not work on the good? Have you tried it?"

"How do you think my mother died? The better question is, how did you know of this plant and what it does?"

"As you said before, I am clever."

"Clearly. Would you care for some tea?"

Maleficent let out a peel of laughter at this. "I'm sorry for my outburst, but you would have to think me completely daft if you really believe I would drink or eat anything you offer me after telling me you poisoned your mother."

Now they were both laughing.

"So, I guess my clever plan just won't work. That is a shame," said Maleficent after she had recovered her breath.

"Well, just because it didn't make her a dark one doesn't mean that you can't still use it to kill Mother Goose. She just won't be evil first. You know, if we poke around the garden, we may be able to come up with a few other ideas, if you want to be more creative. Let's head outside and take a look-see." Hecuba stood and walked to the back door that was indeed the only entrance to the garden. She pushed open the door and motioned for Maleficent to go through ahead of her.

Maleficent exited the hut with trepidation. What new messy hell would she find in this garden of darkness?

To her relief and surprise, it was stunning. A lush garden full of mysterious and exotic plants. Some looked ordinary and others were extravagant. It was beautiful. After taking a few steps, she turned back to make sure that she had not imagined the ramshackle hovel she had just come from. The shack remained unchanged and was, in fact, a blight on the landscape of the impeccable garden she was standing in. However, that was not the most shocking thing that took her aback when she turned. Where she had expected to see a gnarled and withered decrepit old woman, stood a statuesque and slender maiden with flaxen hair cascading past her shoulders.

Maleficent's thoughts must have read clearly on her face, as the visage she assumed was actually Hecuba laugh. Yet this was not the cackle of the old woman from inside the cottage; this was a whimsical chime gently floating on the breeze.

"Hecuba?"

"Yes, indeed." Her voice lilted as if a mere statement was a song and the plants leaned towards her as she walked by them. "I know it can be a little surprising at first."

"Is this the real you, or is the old crone from the hovel the real you?" Maleficent asked after regaining her composure.

"They are both the real me. But in the sense that you mean, I am the crone. For now, let us put that aside. I will give you a tour of my garden and introduce you to my children."

They strolled side by side. Each plant type had a section of its own. When Maleficent asked about this she was told that many of them did not play well with others and had to be kept separate. Much like people, they thrived when they were given their own space. At each section they stopped at, Hecuba would tell Maleficent the name of the plant and what it did. The winsome witherer was a dark purple plant with large pillowy leaves that looked as much like it was made of shadow as actual substance. Upon closer inspection, the inviting leaves had almost invisible thorns peppered across the top. It worked much like the magic spindle. When pricked by the thorn, the victim would fall into a deep dreamless sleep. Unlike the cursed spindle, they would continue to age and wither until they either were woken or turned to dust.

Next was the Woeful Crier, a shrub of white, cascading flowers that looked like small, glowing teardrops. They glistened in the light and gave the visual effect of a weeping bush. One drop of the nectar of this plant and the person would fall into a deep depression. They would cry for days on end and literally die of dehydration.

And so they went, Maleficent learning of twisted roxen and fire flox, binge blossom and wolf mint. Until finally they arrived at a plant with the look of the rampion that was so popular.

"This I assume is the Herminia, as you called it?" Maleficent asked as she fingered one spiked flower.

"Why yes, it is. Now out of all of the things I have shown you today, which is it you would be interested in taking home for your diabolical purposes? Do you still have your heart set on the rampion for the bitter poetry of it all?"

"You have given me a great number of creative ideas on our walk, but yes, I do enjoy the idea of this being her downfall. Tell me, did you supply all of the dark ones with this?"

"Oh no, don't be silly. This plant has been finding its way to them since long before I was born, just as it found its way to me. I just make it easier when and where I can. It doesn't need me or anyone at all."

"I see. Shall we discuss payment? I have no first born to give you so I am at a loss on what tender witches use these days."

"Let's not discuss such things in front of my beauties like they were chattel. It's insulting. Let's go back inside and we can find a deal that will work for both of us, then you can be on your way. I am not a fan of entertaining, and even if I was, you were not invited in the first place."

"Right you are. I do apologize." Maleficent let Hecuba shoo her back into the foul hut and found, much as she had suspected, Hecuba had once again become a disgusting figure, wheezing with every movement.

"Tell me, Hecuba: what do you want from life?" Maleficent asked.

Hecuba took a deep, rattling breath. "Well, I have always wanted to see..."

Before she finished the sentence, she was gone. A shiny, black, scaled claw swiped through her throat before she even knew it had happened. She dropped to the floor into a growing pool of deep red blood. Maleficent found a rag that looked cleaner than the others in the house and carefully wiped her claw clean before it transformed back into a sharp fingernail on an elegantly long finger. She was glad that she had not heard the woman's last wish. She hoped that Hecuba had lived long enough to hold that wish in her heart briefly before realizing that it would never come true, that her dying moment was full of only regret. Maleficent reached into a cape pocket, pulled out a pair of gloves she had brought with her, and put them on. Once back in the garden, she found a trug and a knife and went to work harvesting a basket full of the Herminia.

Maleficent returned to Mother Goose's cottage with a renewed appreciation for the dwelling. Though she may not appreciate the aesthetic choices of Daisy, at least it was clean and had a fresh citrus smell. She marched, unannounced, into the parlor where Daisy and Basil were sitting by the fire talking, and Jacob and Wilhelm were reading. She dropped the basket of Herminia onto the floor between all of them. Every eye turned from the basket to Maleficent in time with each other as if it had been rehearsed.

"This is your rampion impostor. Hecuba calls it Herminia after her mother. I would not recommend any of us ingesting this, as it was used to kill its namesake. It does turn them into dark ones, but only if they already have a small glimmer of darkness in them. It seems it will not take root in someone pure of heart. She was not the primary source for it, though. It grows where it will and always finds a way. I brought these samples back so that you could test them or use them in some way."

"And what of Hecuba? I assume she did not just let you leave with this," said Basil.

"She did not argue about it," Maleficent smirked to herself.

Wilhelm piped up, "So you killed her?"

"Smart lad, someone give the boy a cookie," Maleficent said and ruffled his hair. Wilhelm squirmed away. She made him very uncomfortable, even though he knew that she was on their side. He had the distinct feeling that if someone was in her way, it would not matter to her what side they were on.

Basil ignored the interaction and continued as if no one had spoken. "We will need to get someone out there right away to eliminate the vegetation that grows there. I assume that it is all evil in nature?"

"Of course it is, Basil. Even her thyme was demonic."

"You certainly seem chipper," Daisy said in a reproachful tone.

"Of course I am. I completed the task, got the goods, and vanquished an enemy. It has been a good day, Daisy. Now, Basil, you may want to look at some of those plants for future use. Some of them seem like they could be very helpful."

Daisy gasped. "But they are evil, Maleficent! We do not work with evil."

"Oh, don't we though?" Maleficent interjected slyly.

Basil stepped between them. "We will be destroying all of the plants and I think I have just the person to handle this matter. Daisy, I will need you to contact Mary Mary. After she disposes of the evil, she will live there. It was once the home of the most magical and pure plants in all the world, plants of healing and hope and love. Mary Mary will make it her job to bring it back to its former glory. I have seen her current garden and she is by far the most qualified for the task. Her skill combined with a natural power place can't miss." He then turned to Wilhelm and Jacob. "As for you two, you now have a new job. You will comb through all of the information on all of the current dark ones and those suspected of being dark ones. You will make a record of which ones have a connection to the Herminia plant. When you have completed this, bring the list to me immediately. I have a plan to sort them out quickly and get the ones who are just naughty to safety. Daisy, we are going to need The Piper at the ready."

"The Piper?" Daisy asked.

"Of course you daft-" Maleficent was hushed by a withering glance from Basil. She turned to Jacob. "Perhaps you can enlighten her, boy. I am sure you have already read through all of the staff files, as well as the dark one files. Why would Basil want The Piper here? Come now, prove that you were worth saving and worth the effort to raise and train up with the magical creatures, mortal. Show us how clever you are."

"Well, I assume that he would like the piper to use his magic to lure the non-effected children away from the battle when the time comes. Not only will it keep them from getting hurt and give them a chance at salvation, but it will also make for fewer enemies on the field and probably rattle the ones that remain.

"Well said, Jacob," Basil quacked with pride. "Happy, Maleficent?"

"Ecstatic," she said as she rolled her eyes. "Now that Daisy and the boys have their tasks, what am I to do?"

"Go home and get ready for the coming war, I suppose."

"The war isn't coming; it is here, and the first battle is about to begin. But we have no organization. We do not have an army; we have a pack of individuals with no leader or coordination. How do you think that will play out? Gretel is smart. She has had them training. That is why they attack the villages and raid the fairy glens."

"What do you suggest, then?"

"I suggest we start training soldiers and we all make ready for war. They have the trolls now. Did you notice that? And let me guess. You are the ones that handed them over."

"We did not hand them over," Daisy interrupted. "They were supposed to be raiding the castle."

"You sent trolls on their own with no one to be accountable to? You handed them over."

"As much as I hate saying so, Maleficent is right," Basil said as he paced the room. "We are not an army. When faced with a battlefield, we will all fight bravely but chaotically. It looks like you have a new job, Maleficent. You are now our general. Train them. Make them work together and make them strong. You don't have every long. Can you do it?"

"I truly don't know, but I will very much enjoy finding out. We will need a place to train. They should also all be housed together. We can use my castle."

"No!" cried Daisy.

"Why not? The decor not to your liking? I could hang new drapes."

"We shall speak with King Fredrick about using his castle and training his army as well, joining forces. His people are just as much in danger as the rest of us, and he has more than enough room in that palace," stated Basil plainly.

"Why can't we just use my castle? It is perfectly suitable for our needs."

"If I might?" ventured Jacob. "It would be very good to have more men even if they are non-magical. Sheer numbers will help as distraction and shifting focus of the attackers if nothing else, giving the magical beings the ability to concentrate on their spells and specialties. Remember, the kids we are going against may be well trained, evil, and have some magic items, but they are themselves all humans; perhaps they have more talents or are more gifted than most, but they are still mortal. Also, training the magical creatures with the non-magical ones would build a sense of community and camaraderie that does not currently exist. Speaking as a mortal who was raised by other mortals, you are all respected greatly but also feared, even the good ones. Everyone working together could be good for us in the short and long term."

"Well done, boy," sneered Maleficent. "Maybe you should make one of them Mother Goose instead of Daisy here. You wouldn't get stuck spending as much time explaining things. How well do you make tea, child?"

"That's quite enough, Maleficent!" Basil said angrily. It was rare that he raised his voice and partly because it was a comical sound - a goose trying to yell. "You have a job to do. Don't be petty because it is not exactly where and how you want it. Will you do it or not?"

"Of course, what else have I to do? It actually sounds like quite a lot of fun."

"You do know that you aren't allowed to kill or maim them, right?" he continued.

"Oh, I did not know that, but I do now. I suppose I have some planning and packing to do and you have a King to convince . . . unless you would like me to do that part?" she smiled sweetly. It was unsettling to everyone in the room.

"Daisy will be in contact with you when it is time for you to go."

"Well, this has been quite an evening, hasn't it? I am sad to see it end. Sleep well." Maleficent glided from the room and a moment later, they heard the front door to the cottage slam shut. They let out a collective sigh, looked at each other, then began laughing.

"I didn't even know I was holding my breath till now," laughed Daisy merrily.

"But aren't you upset?" asked Wilhelm after they had all composed themselves. "She called you stupid and made fun of you the whole time she was here."

"Oh Wilhelm, I have listened to her say those things for decades. At least now she is saying them to my face. I choose to find them amusing instead. It works rather well."

"Daisy," said Basil. "You are kindness and grace itself. You make us all better. Thank you. Now I need you to contact Mary Mary, The Piper, and a King. Boys, I believe you have work to do as well."

They all scattered, leaving Basil alone by the fire. He was tired. So very tired. He stared into the fire and tried not to think of anything. It did not work.

Rose ran into the gingerbread house without knocking.

"What do you think you are doing?" shouted Gretel from her desk.

"The witch, Hecuba," Rose gasped to catch her breath.

"The one who supplies us with poisons?"

"The very same. I was just there to pick up some more silent serenade and wormwood and she is dead."

"Oh dear. I assume that means her garden is unattended. But if I know Mother Goose, it won't be for long. Thank you for coming to tell me so quickly."

Rose nodded and turned to leave, but stopped when she felt cold metal against her throat. She slowly looked to her right and Red was standing there, quiet as death, holding the other end of a dagger.

Gretel spoke matter-of-factly. "Never ever barge in here without knocking again. I don't care if the whole bloody castle is on fire. You knock. Now leave."

Rose rushed from the room faster than she had originally entered it.

"Well, isn't that interesting? It took them long enough to get to her."

"Hmmm, I bet Jacob had something to do with that," Red said without thinking.

"Excuse me?" Gretel's voice was dark.

"Well, it's just that if he was spying for us but betrayed us, he must have been spying for them. I assume that he gave them a bunch of information about us and that was probably one of the things he passed along." Red waited to see if Gretel took the lie.

After a short pause, Gretel spoke again. "I see your point. That would make sense. He certainly wasn't very good at getting information to us."

"I will get Snow to form a party to claim the garden as ours and set up defenses. It is unfortunate, but we will need to leave some guards there. I would say we could just harvest everything, but I think we need to consider a long-term solution for this one. Who is best with plants? Actually, Snow is excellent with animals. Maybe that extends to plants and we don't really need her recruiting as much anymore . . . No. I have it! Peter, that boy who likes pumpkin. He has giant ones he has been growing here. I imagine he could do wonders with magical plants in a magical location. I will send him and a few others there right away. Do you think that Bartholomew would be willing to part with a troll?"

"You," said Gretel.

"What?" Red was very confused.

"You will be the one who goes. You are the escort. Help them take it if needs be and set up; then when you are confident it is secured, come back."

"Me?" Red could not hide her confusion and concern. "Why?"

"Because I am telling you to. You should be packing. No telling how long you will need to be there."

Red left the cottage very confused. Gretel was beginning to wonder how much she could really trust her most trusted counsel.

Red and her small band of marauders arrived that afternoon at the broken down, filthy hovel. She desperately hoped that they could be in and out of there quickly and without bloodshed. She had not had time to contact Mother Goose before their departure. It looked empty so she ordered guards to set up in the tree line and Peter to have a look at the garden and make a list of things he would need to make the shack hospitable for him long term. She herself quietly slipped away into the woods. When she considered herself at a safe distance, she pulled out the little pocket mirror and said, "Mother Goose".

The response was rapid as usual.

"Why, good day, Nora. How may I help you?" It was clear from her tone every time they spoke that Mother Goose did not trust or like Red at all.

"I have news. The witch Hecuba is dead but I assume you probably are aware of that. What you don't know is that Gretel has sent myself and a handful of others here to claim the garden as our own. Rose Red had been receiving supplies from Hecuba for a while, it seems. We are here now."

"Nora, where are you personally at this moment?"

"In the woods a little way away from the shack . . . Why?"

"You must stay there and hide."

"But I can't just leave them alone there . . . I need to-"

"For Jacob's sake, hide girl, NOW!"

The mirror went dark. Red stood silently listening. At first, she heard only the breeze, and then she heard them, a group of travelers she had to assume were magical and sent by Mother Goose. Red quietly made her way into a tree that would give her protection, as well as a good vantage point to see what happened. She was going to have a hard time explaining why she was not with them when the fighting happened. Red would have to hope that the good guys won this fight, so she wouldn't have to explain her absence to Gretel. She was clearly already on shaky ground.

Red watched the whole thing play out from her perch. Something odd happened, though. Whenever someone from team good was about to be killed, they vanished. It happened three different times. On the last one, she noticed the fairy reach for something on their chest, and then they were gone before the finishing blow landed. The rest of the battle was fairly gruesome. All involved were fighting wildly, but the inability to permanently take out a foe was draining morale. Mother Goose's people took down every last one of the Children's rebellion, including Peter. Red sat in her tree and waited for nightfall. She knew it would not be safe for her to pass till she could do it unseen. She doubted that Mother Goose had let them know that she was on their side.

When it became dark, she quietly climbed down the tree and stretched her cramped muscles. On her return to the castle, she began considering the story she would tell about her survival. It would have to be very convincing. She also looked entirely too clean and unscathed.

She paused in her journey to contact Mother Goose again.

"I am alive. I just thought you should know," Red said with a bitter edge to her voice.

"Oh, good. Safe travels back."

"Wait. What are you going to do with the garden? Are you going to destroy it?"

"I don't think you need to know that, dearie. Run along home now . . . unless you think it is too dangerous being the only one still alive. If that is the case, we can certainly have someone meet you and get you to a safe place."

"No, that isn't needed," Red found herself saying, even though she desperately wanted to leave and see Jacob. It was clear from Mother Goose's conversations with her that she was not yet redeemed. She would have to stay on a bit longer. "I just need to come up with a good reason for surviving and being relatively unharmed."

"Well, thank you for the information, and again, safe journey." The mirror went blank.

Red arrived back at the castle. She had jogged the last half miles so that she would be out of breath when she arrived. Remembering what had happened earlier that day when Rose had burst in unannounced, she banged on the candy door and waited. Finally, after what felt like an eternity, but was probably less than a minute, she heard Gretel call to enter.

"Red! I certainly did not expect to see you back here so soon. Does that mean that setup was far easier than you had thought it would be and we are all set?"

"No, we were ambushed by Mother Goose's people. I am the only one that made it out, but I do have information that could help us."

"Really? Do tell."

Red was growing concerned for Gretel's lack of concern for her health.

"Well, every time we tried to kill one of them they would vanish. I think they have some sort of amulet or talisman that they all wear that can transport them away when they are in danger. We will need to find a way to deal with that quickly. I bet Bartholomew probably has one that you could study."

"Excellent thinking. You look well. How is it that everyone else died but you look so well?"

"I'm fast and stealthy, you know that. I stick to the shadows and strike when it is safe."
"True, I have always admired that about you."

"Am I missing something? Did something happen while I was gone? You are not acting like yourself, Gret."

"Oh, I am very much acting like myself. You, however, have been acting very strangely lately, so much so that I was worried for you. In fact, I decided that I would be heartbroken if anything happened to you on that mission that I admittedly sent you on out of spite, and a little bit of lingering jealousy over Jacob. I sent a helper to keep an eye out and watch your back. Rapunzel? Would you come out here please?"

Rapunzel stepped out of the shadows silently, even more silently than Red could have done herself. She had no idea that the quiet, mousy girl was a master of stealth. Things were about to get very bad for Red.

"Can you imagine how upset I was to hear about what actually happened today?" Gretel asked rhetorically. "My dearest friend, the girl I called my sister, my right hand. I trusted you with everything. EVERYTHING!"

Red's eyes did not leave Gretel's enraged face. She had never seen Gretel get truly angry, and it scared her.

"I almost wish you had run away to be with your little boyfriend and that damn Goose lover. It hurts me so much to know that you betrayed me. I loved you! You will never be able to understand what that means. Now I have to hurt you, and it has to match the betrayal I feel. Your pain must exceed my pain. Hansel!" At her beckon, Hansel emerged from the adjoining room with a revolting smile spread across his face. "Take her to the dungeon. Make sure she cannot escape; you know how tricky she can be. Get a lot of sleep tonight, Red. Tomorrow you will feel my pain. Now everyone - leave me."

After the room had cleared, Gretel stood at the crystal ball and willed it to life. "Mother Goose!"

Daisy appeared immediately. "Gretel, I assume you have heard of the event at Hecuba's garden."

"I have, but that is of little importance to me. I need to speak with both you and Jacob Grimm."

"Jacob Grimm? Why would you call me to speak with him, Gretel?" Daisy said, clearly surprised and flustered.

"Stop with the games, you old quack. We both know that both Grimm boys are with you under your protection. I need to speak with Jacob now. I have information that you are going to want to hear but I will not relay it until he is here to witness it as well."

A few moments later, Daisy returned with Jacob in tow. "We are both here, Gretel. Now, what news?"

"Your little Red is the subject tonight. I know what she has done to me. Betrayal, spying for you, pretending to care for me as she would a sister. And in truth, I did care for her more than my own family. This wound is deeper than any I have known or anything you could have done to me physically. I am sickened by this level of deceit. She is currently in my brother's care, and I think you know enough about him to know that is not going to be a healthy place for her. I suggest you meet me at the crossroads at dusk tomorrow. I will bring Red; you bring the list I asked you for. Maybe when it is someone you know and care about, you will make a wiser choice. I actually hope that you fulfill your end of the bargain. I love her too.

"Jacob, you should have left her alone. This ultimately is on your head. Everything was fine before you came and started filling her head with ideas of redemption. As much as you want to believe she can be, she cannot be redeemed. She is mine, not yours. Good night. Sleep well. I will see you tomorrow."

Now that she finished her declaration, Gretel could mourn the loss of her friend privately. No one would ever see her tears.

"We have to save her!" Jacob shrieked in a panic. "She has been helping you and that is what got her into this mess: trying to do the right thing this whole time. Give them what they want. We have to do something."

"And we will, my boy. We will bring them locations as they ask. You will stay here, though. I couldn't have anything happen to you. You have proven to be most valuable and you have work that needs to be completed. Plus, I like you and want you to stay safe. This is hard but we will do as they ask. Nora will be here tomorrow evening, we will patch her up, and have a nice cup of tea together. Speaking of tea, drink this." Basil nudged a cup on the table towards Jacob. He did as he was told and drank dutifully. The events of the day weighed heavily on him and he felt himself begin to droop, his eyes sagging with emotion or fatigue, but he could not tell which. And then, nothing.

"Good, now that he is unconscious, throw away that tea so that we do not confuse it with one of our cups. Did you give him enough, Daisy?"

"He will be out until sometime tomorrow night. That should be more than enough time for us to figure out what is to be done."

"Is he going to be okay?" asked a very concerned Wilhelm.

"Your brother will be perfectly fine, but there is no chance that Gretel will release Nora. She will likely be dead by sunrise and we can't risk your brother doing something crazy for the sake of love. She seems like a lovely girl and she has been a great aid to us. We will honor her memory when the time comes, but we must not let our emotions and loyalties get in the way of the goals for the greater good. It is what makes us different from them," said Basil. "Now please help Daisy take your brother up to your room and make sure he is in a comfortable position. He certainly will have a headache when he wakes up. Thank you, Wilhelm. You are a fine young man, and so is your brother."

Daisy and Wilhelm carried Jacob to his room, laid him on the bed, and covered him with a blanket.

"Is there truly nothing that we can do for Red?" Wilhelm stared at Daisy with pleading eyes.

"There truly is not, and I am so sorry. I was a bit curt with her last time we spoke as well, and I regret it so."

"How are we going to tell Jacob? I don't know if he will be able to get over this."

"He is strong and he will overcome it. He will need you and useful work to occupy his mind and make it through."

Wilhelm nodded. He left only for a moment to bring in the work that he and Jacob had been doing and gave it to Daisy. "We were going to give this to you tomorrow morning, but I might as well do it now. It sounds like you will be very busy tomorrow. It is a complete list of those who were exposed to the Herminia and those who were not."

"Thank you so much. This is the biggest help you could have done. Out of curiosity, which list is Nora on?"

"She has never been in contact with Herminia. She is not a dark one."

Daisy sighed deeply and left, closing the door behind her. It would have been so much easier if Nora had just been on the other list.

Red did not sleep. She sat quietly, reflecting on her life and the choices that had lead her here, to this cell. It was empty. She was granted no last meal, as they were afraid she would find a way to escape if they left even a crust of bread with her. She stared at the cold floor and waited. The night seemed never-ending and painfully quiet. They had already either exterminated the other captives or sent them into the labyrinth, so she was the only survivor still in jail.

She heard a door open in the distance and heavy, careless footsteps headed her way. It was likely Hansel. She prayed it was not Hansel, though. He hated her so much.

Lo and behold, Hansel appeared from around the corner. He looked so smug and happy.

"We demanded Mother Goose give us a trade for you. Surprisingly, the old bat did it. Now we have who we asked for, we could give you back . . . but let's let someone else decide, shall we?"

Jacob came into view.

"Jacob! What are you doing here? You have to leave. Get out right now!"

Something was not right. Jacob was smiling as well.

"Oh Red, I missed you so much. They let me come talk to you. I was shocked. You see, I have been spying for Gretel the whole time."

"That can't be true." Red shook her head as if it would shake the implications away with it. "What about your brother?"

"Oh, he has no idea. He is still back at Mother Goose's. He will put it together soon enough, though."

"I don't understand."

"I am a dark one. It really isn't that hard to figure out. Now I have something that I need to tell you, and you probably aren't going to like it very much." Hansel opened the cell door and Jacob walked in, backing Red against the far wall. "You were so eager to be liked, loved even. It was clear you were no dark one. I strung you along all that time."

"But why?" asked Red. It made no sense to her at all.

"Because I was bored. It's as simple as that. How could I have known that you would be even more boring than that stupid Cinderella slut that works in the kitchen?"

"You can't mean any of this. I don't know what they did to you, but you love me. I know it."

Then he slapped her hard across the face. "Are you really so stupid that you don't know when you have been used?"

A tear rolled down Red's cheek, which now matched her name. She stared at his eyes. How could they suddenly be so cold and unfeeling? No, that was not true. There was a feeling there. It was disgust, mixed with hate.

"You look even more pathetic when you cry." He spat on her. "Hansel really wants me to let him have his way with you, or at the very least, make your punishment a public affair. But I think I have earned the right to do this myself." Jacob pulled Red into his arms and whispered in her ear. "It's okay." For a brief moment, a glimmer of hope was resurrected in Red's heart. He said it was okay. He was about to whisper his secret plan to her. Then she felt the sharp pain, metal piercing her heart. "I could never love someone as weak and pathetic as you."

When he stepped away, she looked down and saw the hilt of a blade protruding from just under her solar plexus. The shock never fully registered, and then she was gone.

Jacob turned to Hansel. "You were right about her all along, brother." Jacob sat on the floor and removed his shoes. When he did, the shoes became glass once more and where Jacob had appeared, Gretel now sat. "Leave me. I will meet with you at my cottage when I am done. Bring along Goldie and Snow. We have much to discuss before our meeting with Mother Goose."

Hansel left without a word. He knew his sister was upset about Red, and it would be safer for him to just do what she said.

Gretel walked over to the body that used to hold Nora's spirit and toed it with her bare foot. Definitely dead. She knelt down at her side. "You of all people were supposed to be beside me for this battle and this victory. I was bringing you into the new world with me as my top person. All you had to do was be loyal, but you were so ungrateful. I saved you." She removed the knife from Red's ribcage and wiped it on the girl's cape that she always wore. She then used it to slice a piece of hair from her dead friend and walked away.

As she passed Rose in the hall, she stopped, struck with a sudden idea. "Rose, I need you to deal with that." She waved a hand towards Red's cell. "Remove the ears and tongue, sew the eyes shut, and display it in the courtyard with a sign that says 'Traitor'. Do it quickly because it will not have long to be on display. I need it again for an appointment I have at dusk."

"I will attend to it now."

Chapter 7

Daisy, Basil, and Maleficent all waited at the crossroads silently. None of them felt like making idle chit chat. The day was brisk and clear. Gretel, Hansel, and Goldie emerged from the wooded path in front of them with a wagon in tow.

After a few moments of staring at each other, Gretel spoke first.

"Pleasure to finally meet you face to face, Mother Goose. I assume that you did not live up to your end of the bargain, and still have no intention of giving me any information."

"Of course," said Daisy. "And I assume that Red is already dead and laying in that wagon behind you."

"Of course. I will leave her with you as a good will gesture. I think we both know why we came to this meeting."

"To finally end this."

"Yes, I think we have both grown weary of the back and forth. You set the time and I will choose the place."

"Two days from now, at dawn."

"Fine. We will meet on the field of Bramhoff."

"Really? Not your castle where you are protected and we would need to lay siege, exhausting our troops?" asked Daisy, genuinely surprised.

"I don't need an advantage for this. I am better prepared and just smarter than you in general. I will crush you fairly."

"Very well. We will be there."

"Oh, just as a kind bit of advice, your amulets will no longer work. That just wouldn't be fair."

Hansel brought the wagon forward and then the dark ones left. When it was certain they were gone, Maleficent walked to the cart and removed the cloth covering Red's body. Not only had the main sense receptors been removed or altered, but the body was covered in rotting eggs. She suspected it had been left out as target practice for the others.

"Well, they certainly made it clear how they feel about traitors. You probably shouldn't look, Daisy." She threw the fabric back over the body. "Also, I have to say I am impressed. I did not think you would be able to keep such a calm and cool exterior. Well done. Good show."

"Maleficent," Basil began, "I appreciate that you are beginning to gain a little insight into why Daisy is an asset to our team; however, I suggest our journey back be a time for silent reflection."

The trio traveled on in silence until they arrived at the cottage. Wilhelm was waiting for them at the door. "I'm glad you are back. Jacob woke up and I didn't know what to do so I tied him to the bed. I was afraid he would do something crazy and get himself hurt."

"Daisy, I think this requires a gentle touch. You would be the best to deliver the news to him and keep him calm. Let him grieve. Maleficent and I will discuss the coming battle, but we will be right in the parlor if you need assistance. Wilhelm, please go with Daisy." Basil dismissed them to their chore. Then he and Maleficent retired to the parlor to discuss their plans.

"Oh Basil, that Gretel is so full of hubris. It will be very useful for us during the battle. It is hard to believe that she picked a fair playing field. I was suspicious of that until she continued talking about how amazing she is."

"I'm dying, Maleficent," Basil blurted out.

"Excuse me?"

"I am dying. I have known for quite some time. I was hoping that I would at least be able to hold on through this conflict, but I fear I am done."

"Does Daisy know?"

"No, but I need to find a way to tell her tonight. She will need to continue on as the face of this army, to be strong and lead the others into the fight, but I need you to make the choices she cannot. But you must be kind to her. You need her kindness to temper your . . . temper."

"I understand. When do you think it will happen? Are you afraid? How old are you?"

"I am very old, too old, in fact. But I am more afraid of what will happen to all of you when I am gone. Tomorrow morning, I will go to the pond and watch the sunrise. Now if you do not mind, I would ask that we say our goodbyes now. You have a lot of work to prepare for and I have some thinking to do."

"Of course. Sleep well, my friend."

Maleficent swept from the room and refused to look back. As much as she was annoyed and confused by Basil and his choices, she respected him and considered him to be one of her only true friends.

After a few minutes, Daisy came down the stairs and sat on the settee near the fire. She picked Basil up into her lap and rested her hand on his back.

It was comforting to both of them. They had been together a long time now, since Daisy was 16. He looked at her as he had not done in ages. Her hair was no longer blonde but gray, but not that dull, lifeless gray many people's hair turns. It was more silver than gray, shining in the firelight. She looked tired. He was tired too.

"How did it go, Daisy?"

"As well as could be expected. At least he is not going to bolt or do anything stupid. His brother is comforting him now. It will be a late night for them both. How did things go with Maleficent? Did you get it all planned out?"

"Yes, everything is in order. Well, almost everything. Daisy..." Basil hesitated.

"What is it, Basil?"

"Have you enjoyed your life?"

"What do you mean?"

"You could have done anything, but you chose to stay here with me and take up the mantle of Mother Goose. You forsook having a family and adventures of your own for this."

"Oh Basil," Daisy laughed, "of course I have enjoyed it. I do have a family. You are my family, and now the boys as well. We have had so many adventures, and you made it possible for me to make a difference in this world. Why are you asking this now?"

"Because this is our last evening together, Daisy, and I want to make sure that I have done right by you."

"What are you talking about? Are you sending me away for some reason?"

"I am dying, Daisy."

Tears brimmed at Daisy's eyes. She had been feeling that something was off for a while now and had managed to push it all down in the midst of the war they were dealing with.

"What? No. Don't be silly. You look fine, Basil. You just need a good night's sleep."

"Daisy, you know I am right. I have been here for so long. I was hoping to at least see you through this battle, but I can't. I'm done. Let's just sit, enjoy the evening, and not think of things like war."

"Alright, Basil. Whatever you want, my dear."

They sat together reminiscing and laughing until Daisy fell asleep near dawn. Basil said a quiet goodbye to his best friend and waddled out to the pond. The water was cold but he didn't mind. He watched the sun rise one last time and tried to think about all of the good he had done.

Daisy opened her eyes and let them adjust to the light. She was on the settee and after a brief moment of confusion remembered what had happened the night before. Basil would be gone by now. She heard a polite throat clearing behind her and sat up immediately to see who was in her house. It was Rumpelstiltskin.

"Mr. Stiltskin!" she said in surprise, a bit louder than she would have liked.

"I'm sorry to barge in, Daisy, but I heard about the battle that is planned. I have come to help. Are you okay?" He sounded genuinely concerned.

Tears sprang forth from Daisy's eyes against her will.

"It's Basil," she blubbered. "He's dead."

"What happened?" Rumple was shocked by the news.

"It was just his time. But we talked last night. Tomorrow is the big battle, Maleficent is in charge, but I still have to be the face of this whole thing."

Rumple walked to Daisy and sat next to her. He put an arm around her shoulder and let her cry for a few minutes. "Daisy, we need you to be strong for a little longer. You have always been strong and have managed a brave face for everyone. That is what you need to be able to do tomorrow. Where is Maleficent now?"

"She is training everyone at King Fredrick's castle. His army has joined forces with ours in hopes to put an end to this once and for all."

"Good, it is important that we increase our numbers to match theirs, at least."

"Rumple, there are some things you should know. Bartholomew the Troll King has sided with Gretel. Red was spying for us but is dead now; the Grimm boys live here with me and found a link to how the dark ones are created. So much has happened since you left. I am afraid of what Maleficent will do now that Basil is not around to reign her in. She has never been subtle about her feelings toward me. We need you now more than we ever have. She might listen to you at least a little bit. One of our first priorities has to be to get the kids who are not dark ones out of the path of danger. We have a plan but need to make sure that Maleficent leaves enough time before the fighting begins for the plan to unfold."

"We will make sure it all proceeds as planned. I think we need to be on our way to that castle and have a good long chat with the dragon lady . . . I mean, Maleficent."

Daisy let out a small giggle. She was very relieved that Rumple had chosen today to return.

When Daisy had dressed and grabbed a piece of bread for the road, she and Rumple readied themselves to head to the castle. Before they had made it to the door, Wilhelm came bounding down the stairs towards them. "Wait! I want to go with you."

"Wilhelm," said Rumple. "It's good to see you, boy, and to see that you are well. I would like you to stay that way, which means you need to stay here with your brother. During the battle, we will not have the time or resources to protect you. You will be safe here."

"But I want to see it all firsthand so I can document what happens. Tomorrow, people will need to know what really happened. History will need to know."

"You can't document anything if you are dead, boy."

"I can stay at a safe distance. I can go early and find a spot to hide. Jacob will stay here in case anything happens to me."

"Does your brother know what you are planning?"

"No."

"Then how can you be so sure that he will stay here and wait patiently?"

"He doesn't even know of the battle. All he has thought of is Red. I told him I will be on a journey for the next couple of days to try to help save the other kids who are not dark ones, and he seemed to accept that."

"Mr. Stiltskin," said Daisy, "we can't let him go."

"Daisy, we have no choice. He has earned the right to make his own choices. Hurry up and get yourself ready, boy."

Wilhelm obediently pulled on his boots, threw on a cloak, and grab his satchel, making sure that his journal was inside. With that, they were off to King Fredrick's castle.

"It's time to see if you have earned your position, Goldie," said Gretel from her desk.

"Oh, you will be quite pleased, I think. There was a little bit of a trial and error at the beginning, finding just the right balance of praise and punishment. Not too little, not too much, but just right. I found it, though. Mother Goose is outnumbered and will be out-maneuvered. Shall I send an advance party to scout out the battlefield, and perhaps leave some traps for the big day?"

"No, there will be no need for that. We will win this fairly so that no one can ever contest our victory. There is no way they can stop us. We are better trained to work as a unit, we have plenty of magic, and we are smarter than they are. Look at what we have already accomplished that hundreds of years of dark ones have not. It is our time."

Goldie considered telling Gretel that this was an error in judgment and that although she was confident, they should still take precautions; but a moment of examining the fervor in Gretel's eyes made her stay silent. She could always send someone quietly on her own to do this, instead. Gretel didn't need to know every little thing that went on behind the scenes.

"Alright. I will be on my way. I need to make last minute preparations and talk to the Troll King about his army's part in this. I will leave you to your own devices."

"Please do."

Goldie went to find Snow, Hansel, and Rose. The four had become quite close over the many months that they had been working together as the captains of Gretel's army. Frequently, they took it upon themselves to make decisions they knew Gretel would disagree with, but they knew would work out better in the long run. As long as they stuck together, everything worked well.

"OK, Gretel is not on board with this, but I think we need to someone to the field tonight to set up some traps for tomorrow. Gretel wants to fight fairly in this battle for some reason, but I think we need every advantage we can get. Who wants to do it? I would but I will be busy here with the troops. It' s really a shame we don't have Red anymore; she would be perfect for this."

"So," said Rose, "shouldn't we just send the person who took Red down at her own game, instead?"

Snow perked up at her sister's words. "You are so right, Rose. Rapunzel would be perfect for the job. I can tell her if you want, Goldie."

"That sounds wonderful. Rose, you go with her and help plant the traps that should be set. Hansel, why don't you keep your sister company, maybe talk her down a little. She seems like she is getting into one of her maniacal dictator moods. We need brilliant leader Gretel instead."

"I am on it."

"Thank you, King Fredrick, for joining our cause. I am terribly sorry I was not able to come and formally invite you," Daisy said in the king's drawing room.

"Please, Mother Goose, think nothing of it. These are hard times and we all must pull together. You have done so much over the years to keep us all safe. This is the least we can do. And please, while you are here, call me Freddie."

"Thank you, Freddie. You may call me Daisy if you like." She blushed slightly.

King Fredrick was an older gentleman, still attractive even with the loss of his youth. He and Daisy had many interactions in the past, but none had taken the flirtatious tone that this one had, which seemed odd to Daisy since the circumstances were so dire. Perhaps this was just a relief in a stressful situation. Whatever the reason, it made her feel revived.

Rumpelstiltskin merely rolled his eyes in the back of the room, waiting for the pleasantries to be over.

"I know Maleficent can be . . . forceful at times. I trust she has not made a nuisance of herself or caused too much disruption."

"Well, she is a big personality. No damage has been done that cannot be repaired, though." They both chuckled.

There was a knock on the door and before a greeting was offered, it opened and Maleficent glided through. "I hope I am not interrupting."

"Actually, I was just about to find you," said Daisy.

"I see the dwarf is back on board." Maleficent nodded towards Rumple. "It took you long enough to get over your pride and come help us."

"You are one to talk, Maleficent," the dwarf said angrily. "How long did it take you to come around before you came back?"

"That is enough," Daisy said forcefully. "We are taking up the king's time right now and do not need to embarrass ourselves in the process. Now, where do we currently stand, Maleficent?"

"We have trained soldiers that King Fredrick has kindly provided. Not much had to be done there, as they are well trained. Then we have our ragtag group of magical folks. They have never had to work together before. Though I have tried to get them to function as a team, I am afraid there is not much we can do to remedy that situation before tomorrow. We will just have to do the best with what we have. Oh, and the piper is ready."

"So it looks a bit grim, then?" asked Daisy.

"Extremely."

"Well then, I suppose this is a good time for a cup of tea, followed by a pep-talk to the team."

After they had their tea, Maleficent led them down to the training grounds and called everyone to attention. The soldiers all obeyed and fell in line immediately, but the magical creatures meandered their way over at a leisurely pace, finishing whatever task they had been working on before moving.

"Thank you," said Daisy. King Fredrick was at her side, with Rumple and Maleficent standing behind on either side like sentinels. "I appreciate the dedication you have all shown to our cause: our fight for good. I just need you to work a little harder for a little longer. You need to work together if we are going to make this happen. It is no longer about each individual. It is about all of us. I will be there with you tomorrow. We will win because we have to."

A cheer went up in the ranks of the humans, and gradually, the magical minions as well.

"Well said, Daisy," Fredrick whispered in her ear. "Have you ever given thought to a future in politics?"

"When would I ever find the time?"

Rumple and Maleficent joined the rest of the army in training for the remainder of the day and tried to teach them to share and work together. Part of the problem was that each of them had such unique and individual talents, it was difficult to find ways to weave them all together tactically.

Daisy and Freddie headed back into the castle to discuss the long-term effects of the battle, depending on which side was victorious.

"So, where is your goose? He has always been a pleasure to speak with," Freddie asked.

"He passed away recently."

"I'm very sorry to hear that. You seem to be bearing it well." He took her hand in his and led her to a couch to sit. He sat beside her and continued to hold her hand. She felt odd that at her age, someone could arouse her interest in this manner; especially in the dire circumstances that they were facing, and so recently after the loss of her best friend. She had of course often dreamed that one day she would find a companion but dismissed the thoughts as flights of fancy that would never come true. Now the day before a great battle like none the magical community had never known, that hope flickered within her once more. After all, Basil was gone, and she was not magical herself. What would she do after this was all over, if she indeed was still alive? Raise the Grimm boys, perhaps, and host get-togethers and meetings for the magic fold, but she could not continue to be their leader. That was Basil, not her. Who would take his place now that he was gone? Maleficent? Rumpelstiltskin? Maybe it would all just fall apart. After all, they could not even work together for one battle. Hopefully, if they won, there would be an end to dark ones for good. Now that they knew how to track them, they could be kept in check must more easily. The March Hare could take over. He had the knowledge to send people where they needed to be. Yes, that seemed like a fine plan to her.

"Daisy, are you alright?" asked Freddie.

"Oh, I am terribly sorry. I have so many things on my mind right now. It has been a very hard year on all of us. I think the idea of it all finally coming to a conclusion tomorrow, one way or another, has possibly overwhelmed me."

"You are the one who has overwhelmed me, Daisy. All of these years that we have known one another, and we have never had time alone to talk. I regret not having pushed the issue before now. I very much want to get to know you, Daisy. After this is all over, would you be willing to take some time with me?"

Daisy blushed deeply. "Freddie, I think that would be marvelous. You should know that no matter what happens tomorrow, I will still be in the charge of two boys. I have taken responsibility for raising them. I am all they have."

"Of course. I would never expect anything less from you. That doesn't mean that we cannot also make time for each other. I have plenty of people around here who can tend to children and fantastic tutors that can be at your disposal. My own children are grown now, so the tutors spend most of their days studying or writing. They could stand to shake off the dust."

Daisy and Fredrick spent the rest of the day getting to know each other better and decided they were both happy to see where this would take them. They would worry about tomorrow, tomorrow.

Wilhelm arrived at the field as the sun was setting. He was hoping to avoid seeing anyone and take some time to scout out the perfect spot to watch the conflict from. The field was not completely clear. There were areas of trees and large stones scattered throughout which would work to his advantage. If there had only been one or two trees, he would be much easier to spot. He found a particularly full tree for late fall and climbed up to see the vantage point and how covered he would be from view. He found a spot that was fairly comfortable and settled in. He would wait there for a while to see if he could handle being there and still for a long period of time.

After about 30 minutes, the sun had set and it was beginning to get chillier than he was comfortable with. He decided that this would indeed be his hiding place for tomorrow. It was time for him to go back to the castle and get a few hours' sleep before returning to make sure he could sneak into the tree again before others showed up and spotted him. He was certain after the way Gretel treated Red that he would not want any of the dark ones to find him.

He heard a noise and froze in his spot. He listened closely to try to determine whether it was an animal, the wind, or possibly something more sinister. Voices. Those were definitely voices.

He dared a peek out of his spot and saw Snow, Rose, and someone he did not recognize with long golden hair walking onto the field and inspecting the area. They pulled a cart full of various items that he could not clearly identify from where he was. He continued to watch and realized they were setting up traps on the field. Thankfully, he was there to see this, so he waited patiently while noting where each trap was set. When they had finally finished their task and left, he hurried down from his hiding place and went right back to the cottage immediately. He knew that no one would be there, but he did not know the way to King Fredrick's castle or how far it was. He rushed to the crystal ball and then realized he could not use that because Gretel would surely hear him. Then he had an idea. He found Red's body. They had not had time to properly honor her yet, so she was not buried. He felt sickened when he saw for the first time with his own eyes what Gretel had done to her. Suppressing vomit and bile, he rifled through her pockets and was extremely relieved to find the mirror that had once been his brother's.

"Mother Goose? Daisy? Are you there?"

Daisy's face appeared in the mirror. "Wilhelm? What is wrong? Are you alright? Is Jacob awake?"

Wilhelm took a moment to appreciate the sound of concern in her voice. It felt good to have someone who genuinely cared about what happened to him and to his brother. "We are both fine but I was just at the field finding a hiding place, and I found a good one because I was able to watch Rose, Snow and someone else I don't know setting up traps. They didn't see me, but I was able to watch them the whole time. I wrote down where every trap is."

"That is fantastic! That would have indeed been a horrible thing for us to learn of tomorrow."

"But how do I get this information to you?"

"That is easy. Wake the March Hare. He has likely fallen asleep entering files. Have him put this information into the Masterbook. Once it is there, I can read it from the copy I always carry with me.

After that, get some sleep and make sure that you eat a good, hearty breakfast. It is a big day tomorrow."

After performing his tasks, he slipped into bed in the room he and his brother shared. He could hear his brother lightly snoring and took comfort in the sound.

The day broke and both armies had shown up early, taking their time to set up, get armored, and be ready for the impending battle. Mother Goose and King Fredrick would not be fighting but were there as figureheads to sound the charge and inspire their troops. Wilhelm had gotten there before either army and was safely tucked away in his hiding place. He watched as both armies arrived, and studied the differences in their preparations. He also had taken the mirror with him in case he needed to get a message to Daisy.

Gretel was taking stock of her army and feeling extremely pleased with how this was turning out. There was no doubt in her mind that they would win this day. She walked passed Goldie, walking among the ranks and explaining how things would happen. The trolls would be the front wave, brute force taking down as many as they could. Gretel had no interest in the details of battle, so she continued on until she found her brother.

"Hansel, I know you have a love for carnage, but I was wondering if you would stay back here with me so we may claim our victory together when it is done. We will have a great view of the festivities from here."

"Hmmm, I was looking forward to the battle, but I guess watching it would be almost as fun because I could see all of it instead of just what was right in front of me. Plus, there will probably be plenty of prisoners to play with afterward."

"Of course there will. This would be a great thing for us to share, I think, a memory we will cherish forever."

"I would be happy to share this with you, sister. We will enter the new age together."

Both sides began to form ranks and take their places on opposing sides of the field.

On Mother Goose's side, the preparations were lax and chaotic, each individual preparing in their own unique way. It was clear that their attempts at unity had failed. Daisy went on a search for Maleficent before finding her place at the back with the King.

"Maleficent."

"Yes, Daisy? I am quite busy right now, so if you could move it along, I would appreciate it."

"Of course. I just wanted to remind you that you must leave time for the Piper to do his job before anything else."

"I still don't think that it is so important that we get the non-dark ones to safety. They may not be purely evil, but they certainly have all committed crimes at this point that are worth punishing."

"You are forgetting an important tactical advantage that doing this gives us," said Rumple, approaching them from behind.

"And what is that?" Maleficent queried with a raised brow.

"It will decrease their numbers dramatically, about in half, and we need that advantage. It will also ruin the maneuvers they have been practicing. It could be the advantage that we need, considering the disorder we are faced with on this side."

"That is true, and if Daisy had mentioned that as a motivating factor from the beginning, I would have honored her wishes. From now on, we should use you as the interpreter between Daisy and me. It will make life so much easier for everyone," she said, and then noticed the frown on the dwarf's face. "Well, everyone except for you, that is."

"Well, now that we settled that, I will get back to my spot with King Fredrick and practice my big speech. Good luck, Maleficent. Good luck, Rumpelstiltskin. I expect you both at my cottage for tea tomorrow bright and early, so that we may discuss the future after our victory."

Maleficent nodded solemnly, while Rumple showed an uncharacteristic softness and gave Daisy a firm hug before she left.

"What was that for?" Maleficent asked after Daisy had walked away.

"You and I both know that there is a strong likelihood that that tea date for tomorrow is never going to happen. It is entirely likely that for most, if not all of us, we will never see tomorrow, period. It is okay to have an emotion every now and then, especially for someone you have spent so much time with for so many years. Those people are what we call friends. As much as I hate to admit it, you are among those that I call friend." And then he hugged her. She struggled, but he was stronger than she thought, and eventually, she gave into it and realized that it felt warm and good. It was her first real hug. Just as a tear was beginning to form in the corner of her eye, he released her.

"Well, that is just about enough of that Rumple. I am sure you have better things to do with your time. Go yell at someone or something. That is what I am going to do."

The two armies were now in place. All of the rousing speeches had been made. All involved were in a heightened state of anticipation, anxiety, and excitement. Wilhelm watched from his perch as a tall, thin man dressed in brightly colored clothing, topped with a purple floppy hat, walked in front of all those on Mother Goose's side. He walked to the middle of the field and then put a pipe to his lips. Wilhelm knew that this was The Piper, so he quickly inserted the earplugs that Daisy gave him. Though he could not hear when the music began, he could see its effect. As the man played, kids from the Children's Rebellion stopped what they were doing. Some stared at The Piper and others stared at their comrades, trying to figure out what was happening.

About one-third of the children dropped their weapons and belongings and began marching single file towards The Piper. Dark Ones were poking or shaking their friends, trying to get them out of their trance, but nothing stopped the kids from walking towards the piper.

Goldie ordered archers to take out the piper, but by then, the children were surrounding him like a human shield. He marched them all as quickly as he could into the woods and away from the arrow fire. Many children were slaughtered along the way by their own soldiers. The children and the piper quickly disappeared from view into the woods. They would be led to the castle of King Fredrick and locked in cells until the battle was over and they could figure out a more long-term solution.

When he judged it safe to do so, Wilhelm removed the plugs from his ears. The sound of the pipe had indeed faded into the distance. It was clear even from where he was that the dark ones were rattled by the loss of a third of their forces.

It was now time for the battle to officially begin. The wall of trolls advanced on the rag-tag army of Mother Goose. Goldie had informed everyone but Gretel of the traps and their locations in advance so that they would be able to avoid them themselves and also be able to draw their enemies into them. The trolls, however, missed this part of the briefing, which was unfortunate since they were the very first ones to enter battle. Maleficent, however, had made sure that everyone under her command was very well educated on where the various traps were, thanks to Wilhelm and his map. As a result, the first round of fighting went to the good guys. The smaller fairies were able to outsmart most of the trolls and trick them into walking right into the traps. They were not completely unharmed, however, and many fairies were either dead or badly injured.

The next wave began. While this fighting was happening, Maleficent took the opportunity to go rogue, to try to put an end to the whole battle early on, before too many were lost. She transformed into a sparrow small enough to fly relatively unnoticed through the battle. She managed to get behind Hansel and Gretel without anyone being the wiser, and when she was in place, she quickly transformed into a black dragon. Before the siblings even knew what was happening, Maleficent had clamped her powerful jaws on Gretel's head. There was not even time to scream. Her body dropped to the ground at her brother's feet.

Hansel barely processed what had happened, while Maleficent crunched happily on his sister's remains. He caught sight of the fairy godmother's wand that Gretel never traveled without these days. Without a thought to the dragon standing next to him, he dove to the ground and scooped up the wand. Never one to master keeping his temper in check, Hansel thrust the wand in the air and shouted his wish to the heavens. "I wish that magic no longer existed!"

In his mind, magic caused his sister's demise and in his rage, all he could see clearly is that magic had to be punished for causing him pain. He grabbed the wand firmly in both hands and then snapped it. What happened next, he could not have predicted. A great explosion came from the wand. Not only did this kill him instantly, but it caused a ripple of force that cascaded through the battle. Everything that was magic simply ceased to be, not only items and objects but beings as well. All of the fairies, trolls, unicorns, witches, and wizards . . . all of them disappeared.

Even Maleficent. In the matter of an instant, they were all gone, as if they had never existed at all.

As for the dark ones, they had all been touched by magic but were not magic themselves. They did not vanish, but they all died where they stood, their bodies falling to the ground in unison. Wilhelm could not believe what he had just seen. He climbed down the tree as fast as he could, tumbling part of the way. He ran out into the field to see if they were all actually gone. Maybe they had just become invisible. But alas, they were well and truly gone.

After a moment of shock, his mind turned to Daisy. What had become of her? He looked to where he had seen her last and there she stood, mouth agape next to King Fredrick. He ran to her side.

"You're still here!" he cried, clutching her hand. "How is it possible?"

"My dear boy, I have never had a drop of magic in all of my life. I am just as mortal as you. No one ever asked if I had powers; they just assumed I did."

"Does this mean we won?"

"No, Wilhelm. This means everyone has lost. We have lost magic and I have lost my family. I never could have guessed things would go this way."

Wilhelm clutched her hand tightly and Freddie put his arm around her, pulling her close. She felt very cold and very alone. The three of them stood there, staring at the bodies of the dark ones and the empty spaces where their friends had once stood. Fredrick's soldiers stood staring, as bewildered and confused as they were.

That night Daisy and Wilhelm returned to the cottage unsure of what they would find once they arrived there. Jacob was waiting for them and he was clearly very confused.

"What has happened? The cottage changed while you were gone," he said with mild panic in his voice.

They entered the cottage and the once large interior was now an actual small cottage. There was a bedroom, a living area, and a small kitchen. That was all.

"What happened? Where are Rumple and Maleficent? Did we win? Also, the Hall of Records is gone and so is the March Hare."

Daisy sat him down and tried to explain as best as she could, but in all truth, she was still uncertain of what had happened and had no one to ask: Basil, Maleficent, Mr. Stiltskin. They were all gone.

"We will just have to move on with our lives and manage as best as we can now that magic is gone."

Over the next few months, the Grimm brothers spent their days helping Daisy with the chores of everyday life and maintaining the cottage, as well as trying to document every story as best as they could since the records were all gone. The magical journal was also only a memory now. After a time, Daisy and the king became friends, and then, after a brief courtship were married. Daisy, Jacob, and Wilhelm moved into the castle, but it was not long before the boys were men, old enough to be on their own. They frequently visited Daisy throughout the years and reminisced about a life long since past.

Jacob and Wilhelm went on to study the stories of magic in many countries, spending their days documenting as much of it as they could to preserve it forever.

gThe End

Made in the USA
Middletown, DE
14 December 2023

45635381R00109